# TRAPPED at the BOTTOM of the SEA

**Crossway Books by Frank E. Peretti**

*This Present Darkness*
*Piercing the Darkness*
*Prophet*
*Tilly*

THE COOPER KIDS ADVENTURE SERIES
*The Door in the Dragon's Throat*
*Escape from the Island of Aquarius*
*The Tombs of Anak*
*Trapped at the Bottom of the Sea*

# TRAPPED at the BOTTOM of the SEA

WITHDRAWN

## FRANK E. PERETTI

CROSSWAY BOOKS

A DIVISION OF
GOOD NEWS PUBLISHERS
WHEATON, ILLINOIS

*To Joshua and Terra*

*Trapped at the Bottom of the Sea*

Copyright © 1988 by Frank E. Peretti

Published by Crossway Books
        a division of Good News Publishers
        1300 Crescent Street
        Wheaton, Illinois 60187

Cover design: UDG DesignWorks, www.designworks.com

Cover photo: Steve Gardner

www.perettionline.com

Printed in the United States of America

Library of Congress Catalog Card Number 87-71893

ISBN 1-58134-621-2

| DP | | 14 | 13 | 12 | 11 | 10 | 09 | 08 | 07 | 06 | 05 |
|----|----|----|----|----|----|----|----|----|----|----|----|
| 15 | 14 | 13 | 12 | 11 | 10 | 9 | 8 | 7 | 6 | 5 | 4 | 3 | 2 |

# ONE

The morning was warm and clear at Yokota Air Base, near Tokyo, Japan. A C-141 Starlifter, a huge jet transport and one of the prime workhorses of the Military Airlift Command, stood waiting and ready on the apron like a monstrous, winged whale. The cargo was secure, the Aircraft Commander and crew were ready for departure, but the plane's crew door stood open, and its powerful engines remained cold and silent.

Sergeant Al Reed, loadmaster for the flight, stood in the crew door and kept glancing toward the terminal, nervously checking his watch, looking inside the vast cargo compartment of the plane, checking his watch again, then looking again toward the terminal, his expression grim, his fingers nervously drumming.

Meanwhile, inside the aircraft, another loadmaster, Sergeant Max Baker, hastily stowed a bundle behind some shipping crates before anyone else could notice. Then, after drawing a deep breath to relax, he returned to the crew door to join Al.

By this time, Al was getting so jumpy his behavior could have easily attracted attention.

Max came close and said in a low voice, "Hey, Al buddy, you're supposed to look *normal*. Relax."

"We're running late, Max. What's taking Griffith so long?"

"He'll get here, don't worry."

"We're increasing our risks the longer we wait. If we don't get moving right away, there won't be enough daylight when we—"

Max's firm grip on Al's arm made him halt in mid-sentence. Max's eyes carried the clear and very firm message, "Button your lip!"

Al looked down at his feet, drew a deep breath, and tried to calm himself.

Max kept a tight hold on his arm as he said, "I have my 'tools' on board, all set. How about you?"

Al nodded. "All ready. What do you think? The security boys didn't seem to notice."

"Smooth as silk so far. Nobody suspects a thing."

"So what's the holdup in the schedule?"

"Probably Air Force red tape—you know how that is."

"What if somebody found out something?"

Max gave Al a commanding look right in the eyes. "They're *going* to catch on for sure if you don't ease up."

Just then Al saw what he'd been looking for. "Hey, there he is!"

Both men looked across the apron toward the loading terminal to see Colonel William Griffith, a tall and lean officer in his forties, standing just outside the security gate with three other people, obviously civilians: a tall, strong-looking gentleman in a business suit and two teenaged children, a young man and a young lady. The young lady, a beautiful, blonde girl, had some luggage which Griffith picked up to carry for her.

"Oh, *great!*" said Al.

"No, no, it's a mistake. It has to be!" said Max.

"C'mon, you've got eyes in your head, Max! Griffith's bringing a civilian passenger aboard!"

"But it must be a mixup! This is supposed to be a security flight!"

As they watched, Colonel Griffith shook hands with the gentleman and the young man and began to escort the young lady through the security gate and across the apron toward the Starlifter.

"So what do we do now?" whispered Al.

"Everything," said Max with cold eyes. "Exactly the same. C'mon, let's get working."

The two loadmasters returned to their duties aboard the vast transport and managed to look occupied and normal enough when Griffith boarded the plane, escorting the young girl.

"Gentlemen," said Griffith, and the two men gave him their undivided attention. "This is Miss Lila Cooper. She'll be hitching a ride with you back to the States." Griffith went through the introductions, and Lila shook each man's hand. "Be sure to make her comfortable."

Just then, some five feet above them, the door to the flight deck opened and a handsome black officer leaned out and saluted. "Oh, is this the passenger?"

Griffith introduced them. "Lila, this is Lieutenant Isaac Jamison, the copilot."

Lieutenant Jamison stepped quickly down the short ladder and extended his hand. "Welcome aboard, Miss Cooper. We're just finishing our preflight, so as soon as we're all ready I'll take you up to the flight deck and introduce you to the rest of the crew."

Thirteen-year-old Lila Cooper was comforted by the kindness in the lieutenant's eyes. His warmth seemed to be the only thing truly inviting about this big aircraft. From where she stood near the door, the Starlifter looked like a long, tunnel-shaped warehouse full of crates, heavy equipment, and numerous pallets of goods covered with cargo netting, all firmly strapped to the deck for the flight home. The ceiling was cluttered with cables, roaring ventilation ducts, and glaring lights. According to the very sparse and unattractive seating along one wall, it didn't look like they were expecting any guests.

"Max," said the lieutenant, "how about stowing Miss Cooper's bags?"

Max seemed to have his mind elsewhere and awoke abruptly, grabbing Lila's luggage. "Yes, sir. Sorry, sir."

"C'mon," said Jamison, "I'll take you up to meet the crew before we take off."

He showed Lila to the short ladder that led to the flight deck. She climbed up and went through the small door.

Now this was interesting, the very front of the plane where the pilot and copilot sat. It was a surprisingly large area and actually had seating for at least eight or nine people.

Lieutenant Jamison introduced her to the flight crew. "Lila Cooper, this is our aircraft commander, Captain Aaron Weisfield . . ." The pilot, a friendly-looking, surprisingly young man, shook her hand. "Flight Engineer Bob Mitchell . . ." The crew-cutted man turned from a panel filled with instruments, amber indicator lights, and switches and shook her hand. "And our scanner, Jack Yoshita." The strong-looking Oriental had a firm grip and a warm smile.

Lieutenant Jamison began pointing out some of the details on the control panel. "This is the radio . . . well, actually, several different radios . . . and these are the altimeter, attitude indicator, throttles . . ."

But Lila couldn't keep her mind on his quick little tour. She was looking through the windows at the two men who still stood by the security gate, waiting to see her leave—her father and brother. She could see them clearly, but she was hoping they did not see her. She just didn't want to look them in the eye, to face them, even across this distance.

"For takeoff, we'll have you take a seat in the cargo compartment," the lieutenant continued. "It'll be noisy, but as soon as we're underway, we'll give you a good seat right here in the cockpit."

Lila paid attention again just in time to follow Jamison through the rear door and back down the ladder to the cargo area. He showed her to a bench along the wall where she took her place and buckled herself in. There was a small window nearby, but she had no desire to look outside anymore.

"See you after takeoff," said Jamison cheerfully, returning to the cockpit.

And there she sat, thinking that at no other time had she ever felt such a sting of loneliness as she felt right now.

Lieutenant Jamison took his place in the copilot's seat, sliding it forward, buckling himself in, donning the headphones, and turning to the business at hand. All four crewmen began chattering to each other in Air Force jargon as they brought the big plane to life.

As the Starlifter's powerful engines began to whine one by one, Colonel Griffith returned through the security gate to rejoin Dr. Jake Cooper and his fourteen-year-old son, Jay.

"She's all snug and secure," he said with a friendly, conversational tone.

"Thanks a lot, Bill," said Dr. Cooper, his eyes not straying from the big green aircraft now beginning to ease slowly ahead, turning away from them and toward the taxiway.

William Griffith had known Jake Cooper long enough to tell when the man was troubled by something. Usually Dr. Cooper hid his feelings pretty well, but there was always something about his eyes and his tone of voice that could betray a deep, inner turmoil to those who knew him well, and now was such a time.

Griffith felt awkward, not knowing what to say next. "Well . . ." he began, "uh, she should arrive safe and sound at McChord Air Force Base by midnight or so . . . *yesterday!*" He chuckled at the strangeness of that statement, knowing the plane would lose a day crossing the International Date Line.

But Dr. Cooper didn't chuckle back. He couldn't take his eyes or his mind off that big transport moving down the taxiway.

Griffith spoke again. "Uh . . . your sister isn't too far from there, is she?"

Perhaps hearing Griffith speak for the first time, Dr. Cooper finally tore his eyes away from the departing Starlifter and answered his friend's question. "Oh, yes, Joyce lives in Seattle. It's about an hour's drive. Very convenient." He drew a breath, forced a smile, and offered his hand cordially. "Bill, I really appreciate your trouble. I didn't mean for all this to happen at such short notice . . ."

"Hey, don't worry about it. We already had this flight lined up anyway, and one extra body on board won't make a bit of difference among all that cargo."

Dr. Cooper shook Griffith's hand firmly. "Well, thanks a lot."

Colonel Griffith took just a moment to study Dr. Cooper's eyes. "Jake, if there's anything else I can do . . ." It was a serious offer.

Dr. Cooper simply smiled his appreciation. "Well, you can pray for us."

Griffith smiled with kindness and nodded. "I'll do that. And give me a call sometime."

"Right."

Griffith turned and walked away, leaving Dr. Cooper and Jay alone there at the tall, Cyclone fence, just watching that big plane turn around, neither one of them saying a word.

Lila was very quiet as well, just sitting on the bench, waiting for something to happen.

Just then Flight Engineer Bob Mitchell came down the ladder to check up on her. "Hi. Buckled in, I see."

"Uh-huh," she answered, checking her seat belt again.

"Was that your family back there seeing you off?"

"Mm-hm."

"Father and brother?" Mitchell knew that was a dumb question, but he figured he had to make conversation somehow.

"Mm-hm" was all the conversation Lila could produce.

"So . . . is your mother back in the States?"

Lila looked out the window and told him simply, "My mother is dead."

The pain and sorrow in her eyes told Mitchell he'd asked the wrong question, and now he wanted to kick himself.

"I'm sorry."

"It's okay."

He groped around for another subject. "Well, what brought you to Japan?"

"Oh, the government sent us over here as part of a cultural exchange program. My dad's university is exchanging professors with the University of Tokyo for a few months."

"No kidding. What's his field?"

"Umm . . . biblical archaeology, ancient civilizations, that kind of stuff."

"Wow. Pretty impressive. You must be very proud of him."

"I don't know."

Mitchell grimaced to himself. Another wrong question! "Well, I'd better get back to my post. See you in a bit."

The Starlifter paused at the end of the runway, its engines whining, its running lights rotating and flashing. Then, with a thunderous roar, it began speeding down the runway.

Dr. Cooper and Jay watched every inch of its take-off roll, shading their eyes against the sun as the Star-lifter eased off the runway and into the wide open sky, climbing and soaring eastward, out over the Pacific. It shrank quickly into a small black speck trailing a brown smudge of smoke, its roar gradually subsiding, and before long there was nothing more to watch, nothing more to command their attention.

Now the two of them were left alone, and neither could think of what to say first.

"Well, she's gone," said Jay. It was an obvious statement, but he felt it so keenly that he just had to say it.

"Let's get back to the hotel," said Dr. Cooper, walking toward the terminal.

Jay walked beside his father and felt like he just had to talk about what was happening. "This . . . this is really going to be tough."

"What's that, son?"

Jay looked up at his father impatiently. "Well, getting along without Lila. I mean, we've never been apart like this. It's always been the three of us; we've always stuck together. I just don't get it . . ."

Dr. Cooper didn't seem very talkative. "Lila's just going through some things—things she'll have to figure out on her own, that's all."

Jay didn't really want to press the subject, but his feelings just kept pushing out the words. "I'm sure sorry to see her go. Now it's just the two of us; it was tough enough getting used to it being just the *three* of us—"

"We can talk about it later, son."

Jay stopped talking, knowing he'd been ordered to, and he felt angry about it. *We can talk about it later.* He'd heard that phrase before, too many times, and every time his father had that same, hard look in his eyes that Jay could not understand, as if the lively, loving, perceptive eyes Jay and Lila so enjoyed at any other time were suddenly hidden behind a mask of stone. Jay looked up at his father, and yes, those eyes were that way again, almost unblinking, looking straight ahead.

Lila looked out the window, watching the last of the Japanese coastline fade behind them. Now there was nothing below them but an endless flat table of deep blue, featureless ocean.

"You can undo that belt now."

It was Lieutenant Jamison, looking down from the door to the cockpit. He was smiling that same warm smile as he motioned to her seat belt.

"Oh." She released the buckle and stretched a little.

"Come on up and join us."

She stepped over to the ladder and made her way up to the door, where Jamison offered his hand to steady her.

"It's about time for lunch. Would you be interested?"

"Sure." She caught herself. "Yes, please."

"Max ought to be bringing us something shortly."

He offered her a seat on a comfortable bench along the back wall of the cockpit, and then turned to go back to his post.

"Say . . ." said Lila. He looked at her curiously. "Thanks for everything. I've been really rude, I know . . . I'm sorry."

He smiled kindly. It seemed to come so naturally to him. "Hey, we all have our bad days. Just relax now and enjoy yourself."

"Thanks. Oh, and uh . . . Mr. Mitchell?"

The flight engineer looked her way.

"I want to tell you thanks too, and say I'm sorry."

He smiled. "No problem."

Now Lila felt better and took the time to look around the inside of the aircraft from where she sat. Captain Weisfield had switched on the autopilot, and the Starlifter was now flying a steady, level route as he kept a close eye on the controls. The rest of the crew had settled into quieter tasks—some paperwork, some technical talk, a western novel. The atmosphere became relaxed and quiet.

Al and Max stepped out of the cockpit abruptly, apparently having some work to do. She had to admit she wouldn't miss them much; there was just something about them that chilled her, something in their nervous expressions, their stern eyes.

Max finally returned through the flight deck door, carrying several box lunches. The others gave him a cheerful greeting and a few playful whoops over the arrival of mealtime. But Max only managed a forced smile, and even gave Lila a cold stare.

Bob Mitchell dug into his sack and began to lay lunch out on his worktable. "Here, c'mon and share the table," he said.

Lila slid over and took him up on his offer. The lunch wasn't bad: a turkey sandwich, some coleslaw, a carton of milk, and some cookies.

But then she saw Bob bow his head and say a quick, silent prayer over his food.

Lila ventured the question, "Are you . . . are you a Christian?"

There came a cheerful grin. "I sure am."

"Wow . . ." Lila couldn't help showing her very first smile.

"Yeah," said Lieutenant Jamison, "so am I. I'm part of the good ol' family of God at the First Baptist Church in Puyallup, Washington!"

He said that with such a perfect preacher's flourish that she couldn't help giggling.

"Yeah," said Bob, "we're still working on the Skipper there. We're going to get him saved one of these days."

Captain Weisfield looked at them and smiled a wry smile.

"Hallelujah," said Yoshita teasingly.

"Just wait, Jack. You're next."

They all laughed.

Bob seemed much more relaxed. "Now maybe we'll have something we can talk about!"

"Well, amen," said Lila, "because I sure need someone to talk to."

That was the end of the conversation. The very next second, there was a rasping, metallic sound. Bob's eyes became fixed on something behind Lila's shoulder, and his face froze in horror.

"What is it?" she asked.

"Don't turn around," he said in a very quiet, controlled voice. "Don't move."

"Good idea," came a voice behind her.

Lieutenant Jamison turned in his chair and then stiffened. "What is this, Max?" he asked.

Max's voice came from behind Lila, and it sounded cold, cruel, cunning. "This is an Uzi submachine gun, Lieutenant, fully loaded, fully operational. Everyone freeze right where you are."

Max stepped into the middle of the flight deck and immediately had everyone's attention as he held the gun at waist level and swung it to and fro, giving every person a chance to look down the deadly muzzle.

"All of you, hands on your heads, then don't move a muscle!"

The whole crew obeyed. A glance from Lieutenant Jamison prodded Lila out of her stupor of horror, and she did the same.

Max wasn't alone. Now Al appeared in the doorway, also armed with a deadly submachine gun, and looking nervous enough to be very, very dangerous.

"Okay," said Max. "Time for a change in personnel.

Jamison, get out of that chair." Suddenly he shouted, "And no hands on that radio!"

Al held his gun all the more ready in case anyone tried anything.

Lieutenant Jamison slowly slid his chair back and climbed out of the seat.

"All right, you and the girl, out of here! Into the cargo compartment!"

Lieutenant Jamison nodded to Lila, and she got up slowly, a bite of sandwich just lying in her mouth like a lump. She went first down the ladder with the muzzle of Al's machine gun pointing right at her.

"Easy now. No funny business," said Al. "All right, Jamison, you're next. Take it slow."

As soon as Lila and Jamison were well on their way down the ladder, Max got into the copilot's seat, still brandishing his machine gun.

"Now," he said to Captain Weisfield, "we'll just start talking about some course changes."

Al reached the deck of the cargo compartment right behind Lila and Lieutenant Jamison and waved toward the bench against the wall. "Have a seat."

Lila and Jamison sat on the bench, their hands still on their heads.

Suddenly the huge plane banked sharply to the right, giving Lila a very queasy feeling in her stomach.

"We're changing course," Jamison told her.

Al braced himself against the wall to keep his balance during the tight turn. "Looks like Captain Weisfield is doing exactly what Max tells him. Everybody calm down now—just sit tight."

Lieutenant Jamison asked in a very calm, controlled voice, "Al . . . just what is it you're doing?"

Al forced a smile, trying to look clever and in control even though he was obviously very nervous. "This, Lieutenant, is what is called a hijacking. We're taking over the plane."

The Starlifter finished the turn and returned to normal, level flight.

"Where are we going?"

"Oh, somewhere south of here, never mind where. You just worry about yourself and the little girl here. You two are the insurance policy for the flight, you know. One wrong move from anyone up there on the flight deck, and . . ." Al waved the muzzle of the machine gun right under their noses.

Al backed away and stood under the door to the flight deck. "How's it going up there?"

Max's voice came back, "Everything secure. We'll be reporting our position in a second."

Al drew a deep breath and actually calmed down a little "Whew! So far so good, eh?"

Lila didn't hear the comment. She was too busy praying.

# TWO

In the Tokyo Air Traffic Control Center, twenty air traffic controllers were at their posts, carefully watching radar screens and chattering into their headsets as they manned their radio and tracking consoles. When one controller received the call from the Starlifter, it sounded entirely routine.

"Tokyo Control," came the voice through his headset, "MAC 50231, position Rocky, 10:35, flight level 330, estimating 40 North, 160 East. 11:50, 43 North, 170 East next."

"MAC 50231," the controller answered, "Tokyo Control, roger."

Captain Weisfield remained calm and steady as Max shut down the radio. The message Max had just sent to Tokyo told the control center that the Starlifter, "MAC 50231," was heading east toward the United States on its planned flight path, flying at 33,000 feet. Max knew the Starlifter was now out of Tokyo's radar range; they would never know that Max had lied and that the Starlifter was heading south, destination still unknown.

"Nice plan so far, huh?" said Max, chewing rudely on a wad of gum. "By the time we quit broadcasting our position reports, they'll all think we disappeared somewhere up in the Aleutians!"

"So where *are* we going?" asked Weisfield.

"Well, Captain, I'm going to put some coordinates into the navigation system that will take us straight south, between Wake and Guam. The Carolines are nice this time of year, don't you think?"

"What if we don't have enough fuel to reach wherever you're taking us?"

"Oh, don't worry about that. We'll have plenty; I've already figured that out."

"Looks like you've thought of everything," said Weisfield.

"So far, Captain, so far," said Max with a laugh.

The Starlifter flew on, heading south.

Inside the cargo compartment, Lila and Lieutenant Jamison sat very still under Al's gun. Al had finally let them take their hands off their heads, but only after their arms began falling asleep.

Lieutenant Jamison tried to look calm and pleasant as he asked Lila, "How are you doing?"

Lila was looking down at the deck, deep in thought. It took her just an extra moment to come up with an answer.

"I'm . . . I'm scared."

He smiled to reassure her and said, "Hey, that's normal."

"No, that's not what I mean."

He leaned over a little to listen.

Lila looked around as if searching for the words, then said quietly, "I'm afraid . . . well . . . what if I never get a chance to see my father and brother again?"

He touched her hand and said, "Hey, you will. You mustn't worry about that."

She hesitated for a moment and then forced herself to say it. "My father and I . . . we had some very unkind words before I left. I feel terrible about some of the things I said, and . . . what bothers me is that those words were the very last we ever said to each other."

Jamison didn't answer right away. He took some time to ponder.

Finally he said very gently, "It's good that you're thinking about it." Then he smiled. "Funny, isn't it, how trouble makes us stop and think?"

"What do you mean?"

He even chuckled a little. "Aw, you know. The way we humans are, we just keep right on doing what we're doing, even if it's wrong, and maybe we never hear God calling to us until . . . well, until we find ourselves in a jam. *Then* we stop, and we get quiet, and we listen."

Lila wasn't ready for any little sermons. "Well . . ."

"Kind of like Jonah. He tried to run from God, so God brought some trouble into his life to stop him so He and Jonah could have a talk."

"Being swallowed by the big fish, you mean."

"Yeah. Now *that* got Jonah's attention!"

"But hey, listen, I'm not the one who's wrong here. I mean, it's my *Dad* who's the problem!"

He smiled again and said, "Well, only you would know that for sure, but as far as I've ever seen, most fights require at least two people."

Lila just wasn't ready for this. "Can we talk about something else?"

Jamison nodded. "Yes, we can."

He paused for a moment. Al was near the ladder to the flight deck, a fairly good distance from them, and the whole compartment was very noisy with the roar of the engines outside and the rushing of the ventilation system inside. Jamison was content that they could speak without being heard.

"Now don't turn around to look, but do you remember seeing a huge container toward the back of the plane?"

"A big steel thing, like a big bottle?"

He nodded. "Right." He lowered his voice, but still smiled and looked casual as if talking about nothing important. "Lila, that's a special weapons pod for carrying sensitive cargo. It's airtight, watertight, and they tell me it's bullet-proof. It's like a big safe, you understand?" He pointed out the window as if showing her something, and she looked, but he wasn't talking about anything outside. "There's an entry hatch at the other end, toward the back of the plane, and I think it's unlocked at the moment. Now listen to me: if any trouble breaks out, or any real danger—you know, shooting, fighting, anything like that—you get yourself inside that pod and close that hatch. You'll be safe in there until the ruckus is over."

After another hour, Max sent out another false position report, telling the control center in Honolulu that they were on course, heading east, only about an hour west of the Aleutians.

Actually the Starlifter was heading for the Equator, out over the Pacific.

"And that should do it," said Max. He reached down and switched off all the radio equipment. "We'll keep everything nice and quiet from here on out. We don't talk to them, and they don't talk to us."

Within an hour, the control center in Honolulu noticed that MAC 50231's position report was overdue. The controller listening for it waited just a few minutes and then sent out a call.

"MAC 50231, Honolulu."

No answer.

"MAC 50231, Honolulu."

No answer.

The controller called several more times, then contacted the control center in San Francisco.

"San Francisco, this is Honolulu. We're unable to raise MAC 50231, last position 11:50, flight level 330, 43 North, 170 East. Are you in contact?"

"Negative, Honolulu."

The controller called his supervisor. "Ed, we have a negative response from MAC 50231."

The supervisor came over to the console. "That Air Force flight? Any other aircraft in the vicinity?"

The controller checked. "Uh . . . one commercial flight, United 497, from Seattle to Tokyo."

"See if they can raise them."

Honolulu Control contacted the United Airlines flight, and the airliner sent out several calls to the Air Force plane that was supposed to be in the area.

The controller spoke into his headset. "United 497, Honolulu. Any response?"

"Honolulu, United 497, negative," came the answer.

"Better call Yokota," said the supervisor.

The controllers at Yokota Air Base weren't at all happy with the news that their Starlifter had fallen silent. It could very well mean trouble.

Their commander started barking orders. "Phelps, advise 22nd Air Force Headquarters that we may need Search and Rescue. Corey!"

"Sir!"

"Get the flight plan and the manifests for 50231. I want to know who and what's on that plane!" He got back on the telephone. "Keep trying to raise them, Honolulu, and tell San Francisco to stay near the phone."

The Starlifter flew on, and little was said by the hijackers. Al remained at his post, keeping a wary eye on Lila and Lieutenant Jamison. Every once in a while Lila could hear Max talking to the crew in the cockpit, making sure the plane was going where Al and Max wanted it to go, wherever that was.

Then Lila saw something out the window. "Lieutenant . . ."

He looked out the window as well.

They were passing a small island, just a tiny hump in the middle of the vast ocean surrounded by a pale blue shoal and white rings of surf.

Yoshita reported, "Approaching the Northern Marianas."

"Watch it now," said Max, letting the gun barrel give importance to his words. "Just do what the navigation system tells you, and no tricks. I don't want to attract anyone's attention."

Captain Weisfield kept the course even and steady.

"So where are we going?" Lieutenant Jamison asked.

"You'll find out," Al replied.

"I suppose you have your very own airstrip somewhere that's big enough to land this bird."

Al only smiled a wicked smile and said, "Well, let's just say we're borrowing one for the time being. It's an old airstrip the Japanese built during the war. It's in a pretty lonely place; so lonely, I don't think anyone even knows about it."

The man named Corey burst into the Yokota control room with the documents filed for the flight. He handed them directly to the commander, who hurriedly scanned them.

"Oh great . . ." he muttered. Then he said it louder. "Oh, *great!* That's just terrific!" He handed the documents to a lieutenant. "The cargo manifest is classified. Whatever that plane's carrying, no one's supposed to know about it. Are you getting through to the 22nd,

Phelps? We might have ourselves a real problem here."

But then the lieutenant found something else in the manifests. "Hey, we've got another problem. There was a civilian on board."

"*What?*" The commander looked as the lieutenant pointed it out.

"Lila Cooper, thirteen years old, civilian passage to McChord."

"On a classified flight? How did that happen?"

The lieutenant read further. "Uh . . . a government cultural exchange program . . . Her family is still here in Japan . . . Apparently she had to leave abruptly and . . . yes, it was authorized."

The commander paced a bit, stroking his chin, combing his hair with his fingers, turning this way, then that.

"I would say, sir," continued the lieutenant, "that we are looking at a *monumental* embarrassment if we lose that plane."

Phelps had 22nd Air Force Headquarters on the line. "Got them, sir!"

The commander snatched up the phone. "This is Myers. We've lost contact with MAC 50231, en route from Yokota to McChord. We'll get you the last reported position. See if you can raise them or sight them. But get this: The cargo was highly classified. Right. Hang on . . . I have one more for you: There was a civilian on board, a teenaged girl from the States. You're going to have a hard time keeping this quiet, but keep a lid on it, you follow? We'll be in touch."

He set the phone down and tried to do some heavy thinking.

The lieutenant had a disturbing question. "What about the family of that girl?"

"What about them?"

"Should we notify them?"

The commander looked at the lieutenant as if the

question was a stupid one, but then gave it some more thought. "Oh, brother. If we're not careful, we're going to be looking at a breach in security a mile wide." He thought for a moment longer. "No, don't notify them . . . not yet. We still have time. Let's not say any more than we have to . . . to *anyone.*"

Max kept watching every move the flight crew made.

Weisfield was trying to be cooperative.

Suddenly a green light lit up on the center instrument console.

"What's that?" Max demanded.

"Uh . . . it's . . ." Weisfield started to answer.

"We're being tracked!" Max shouted. "Someone has us on radar!"

Bob Mitchell, the flight engineer, tried to explain. "It's just a communication light . . ."

"Don't fool with me!" Max yelled. "I know this plane well enough to know we're picking up a radar signal!"

Weisfield tried to offer an explanation. "It might be the base in Guam picking us up, but I'm not sure."

"Well, get away from it!"

"How? Max, we're out in the middle of flat ocean!"

"Just do it!"

Al could hear Max shouting and stood up. "Max! What's up?"

He wasn't watching Lieutenant Isaac Jamison. It was a sudden move, a very slight chance taken, but Jamison took it. He leaped from his seat and pounced on Al, grappling with him, trying to get control of the gun.

Al kicked, screamed, and hollered as the gun went off like a string of firecrackers, punching an arc of holes in the ceiling and filling the air with pungent smoke. There was a sudden loud hissing of escaping air.

Lila immediately dropped to the floor and rolled behind a pallet of crates for cover, her ears numbed by the blast of the gun, her heart racing with terror.

Max burst out of the cockpit at the sound of Al's cries, saw Jamison and Al scuffling, and screamed, "Hold it, Jamison, or you're a dead man!"

Jamison weakened his grip a little, and it was all Al needed to shove him away. Max tried to bring Jamison down with a burst of gunfire, but then he was suddenly grabbed from behind by Bob Mitchell. Max screamed and struggled and his finger locked down on the trigger, releasing a frenzied volley of bullets that zinged off the metal floor, ricocheted and pinged about the compartment, and traced sparks and blazing streaks through the smoke-blued air. Two bullets hit Jamison, and he fell to the deck. He immediately looked at Lila, his face contorted with pain, and nodded toward the weapons pod.

Max was out of control and kept firing his gun at nothing in particular. More bullets punched through the Starlifter's skin. An alarm began to sound and the compartment lights came to full brightness. The cabin pressure was dropping! Al tried to fire at Mitchell, sending a spray of bullets into the flight deck that punched holes through the control panels and instruments. Mitchell was hit and fell to the cargo compartment floor.

An explosion! Smoking, metal fragments burst through the plane's left side, tearing the plane open. Al disappeared through the hole like a particle of dust into a vacuum cleaner. The Starlifter reeled to one side, then the other, swayed, dipped, rocked.

The crew on the flight deck had grabbed their oxygen masks and were breathing from emergency supplies as Captain Weisfield gripped the controls and tried to keep the plane steady. "Number Two Engine fire!" He immediately threw the Number Two throttle back. "Throttle, idle start." He yanked at a handle above him. "Fire Handle Number Two, pulled. Extinguishing agent released."

Jack Yoshita leaped over to the flight engineer's panel and tried to assess what had happened. "Rapid loss of cabin pressure! The cabin wall is perforated. Some bullets must have hit the engine!"

Captain Weisfield noticed his shoulder turning red from a wild ricochet. He switched on the radio. "Mayday! Mayday! MAC 50231 . . ." The plane began to shudder and slide from side to side. He shoved the control yoke forward and the Starlifter nearly stood on its nose, diving toward the earth. He was trying to get down to a safer, breathable altitude.

Lila couldn't breathe. Her mind was melting away and her vision was going black as she finally managed to grab an oxygen bottle off the wall and slap the mask over her face. Life coursed through her veins, and she awoke again.

But now she was rolling, sliding down the steeply inclined deck toward the front of the plane. She grabbed a pallet with a free hand and hung on. The plane was bucking like an angered stallion. She could look out the gaping hole in the wall and see the big jet engine just outside, now billowing smoke and flame, its side blown open. Some pieces of it were actually lying inside the cargo compartment.

Max had tumbled to the front of the compartment and now lay sprawled on the floor, his face and hands a deathly blue. He no longer held the machine gun. He wasn't moving at all.

Lieutenant Jamison was bleeding from wounds in his chest and hip, and he too had grabbed an emergency oxygen bottle and was gasping air from it. He kept looking at Lila, motioning for her to get to the weapons pod.

She began to climb toward it, gasping from the

oxygen mask, grabbing any handhold she could find. It was like climbing a very steep, rolling, bucking hill, but she was getting closer.

Weisfield was getting weak. He kept the Starlifter in a dive, watching the altimeter, but he could tell the big ship was dying.

"Loss of Hydraulic System Number Two!" Yoshita reported.

"The fire!" said Weisfield. "It's torching through the control lines! We're going to have to ditch this thing!"

The Starlifter was swaying and zigzagging crazily through the air, dropping toward the ocean. They were below ten thousand feet now. Weisfield pulled back on the control yoke and the big plane tried to struggle out of its dive, shuddering and shaking like a broken kite.

"Hang on," said Weisfield, "we're going for a swim."

Lila could feel Lieutenant Jamison's arms around her. He was holding her steady, trying to help her along. The plane had leveled a little, but it was still diving, rocking, swaying, fishtailing. Both of them were praying. They could hear the roar of the air over the plane's fuselage and the loud crackling of the left wing being eaten by white-hot fire. The increasing atmospheric pressure felt like it would burst their eardrums. Lila could look out the window directly beside her and see the cloud layers whisking by them like floors going by a dropping elevator. The ocean was rapidly getting closer and closer.

"Inside, girl, *inside!*" said Lieutenant Jamison, giving her a boost with his hand.

Lila reached and pulled herself up into the large hatch of the weapons pod, rolling into its dark interior. She looked back, but Jamison had collapsed out of sight.

"Lieutenant Jamison!" she cried, scurrying toward the hatch.

He reappeared, struggling to stay on his feet, very faint, very weak. He slammed the hatch shut, and she was in total darkness. She could hear him outside, tinkering with the lock.

Lieutenant Isaac Jamison, bleeding and dying, held himself up with one free arm as he worked the locking mechanism, threw the bolt into place, removed the special key.

Lila lay in the dark, still feeling the Starlifter reeling, swaying, dropping . . .

Impact! The pod lurched and rang like a bell as metal fragments and debris struck against it. She heard the tearing, ripping sound of the Starlifter's skin peeling away, and then the thunderous crashing of water.

Then came the tumbling, the endless rolling, like a stone skipping across the water. She was being tossed about inside the pod like a garment in a dryer, reaching, grabbing for something, anything.

There was one final blow, one final crashing of the pod, and Lila lost all awareness, slipping into a dream.

# THREE

"Yes," said Dr. Cooper in answer to a question, his voice echoing in the large lecture hall at the University of Tokyo, "I would say that the siege engines uncovered at the site were Babylonian in origin."

A graying, dignified Japanese professor was serving as an interpreter and rattled off Dr. Cooper's words in Japanese. Then Dr. Cooper continued.

"The Book of Nahum, chapter 2 and verse 5, refers to them as 'mantelets' and confirms their use in the siege of Nineveh."

More interpreting.

"Just let me add that we ourselves uncovered relief carvings of remarkable similarity—even as far as the structure of the battering rams—at the recent dig at Tell Kuyunjik."

The professor interpreted again.

"So again I would underline that the Bible is shown by such findings to be an accurate and reliable record."

The professor finished delivering Dr. Cooper's answer, and then the two hundred students and faculty in the hall responded with an energetic mutter of approval.

Dr. Cooper was noticing the clock. "And I believe that will do it for today. I'll have those slides to show you tomorrow, and I'm sure by then you'll have some more questions. Thank you very much."

The interpreter delivered Dr. Cooper's final words for the day, and the gathering dismissed.

Dr. Cooper and his interpreter, Professor Nishiyori, stepped down from the platform.

"A fascinating lecture, doctor," said Nishiyori. "The field of biblical archaeology is a whole new world for us."

"A world worth looking into, I can assure you."

"It has been a pleasure!"

"Thank you very much." Dr. Cooper looked at his watch. There was something on his mind. "Uh . . . where can I find a phone?"

"You may use the telephone in my office. Come with me."

In Professor Nishiyori's office, Dr. Cooper placed a call to the United States, to his sister Joyce in Seattle.

"Oh . . . Jake," came his sister's voice, "I was wondering if you'd call."

There was something in her tone that told Dr. Cooper all was not right. "Well, sure, I wanted to check up on Lila, make sure she got home all right. And there's something I really need to talk to her about."

"Well, she isn't here. There was some kind of mixup in the flight schedules or something. I went down to McChord to pick her up, but the plane never arrived. I tried checking with the people at the terminal, but no one seemed to know anything."

Dr. Cooper could only sit there silently for a moment. This wasn't making a bit of sense. "I . . . I don't think I understand what's going on here . . . Did you have the correct flight number?"

Dr. Cooper could hear Joyce rustling through some papers on her desk.

"Okay," she said. "The flight was MAC 50231, inbound from Yokota Air Base. Now is that the right one?"

"Well . . . yes. My records match yours exactly."

"Well, Jake, there's been a foul-up somewhere."

Dr. Cooper sighed and let his head droop a little. "That's the military, I guess."

"Is there something you want me to tell her—whenever we find her, that is?"

"Oh . . . no, not really. She and I . . . well, things weren't very good between us before she left, and I just wanted to patch it all up."

"Well, nobody at McChord could help me, so they're all in the dark and so am I. I honestly don't know what became of my niece."

"Well, tell you what, I'll see what I can find out at my end and you see what you can find out at yours."

"All right."

"You have my number at the hotel?"

"Yes, right here. I'll call if I hear any news."

"So will I. Thanks."

When Dr. Cooper got back to his hotel room, he called Yokota Air Base and went through three or four call transfers before he finally got someone who knew what flight he was referring to.

"Right," said the person on the other end, "your daughter was on MAC 50231. That arrived at McChord today."

"Could you please double-check that?" asked Dr. Cooper. "The news I have from Seattle is that the plane hasn't arrived."

"Well, no . . . that would have to be a mistake."

"Oh, I'm sure there's a mistake, but let's find out where."

They talked a while longer, but Dr. Cooper could tell he wasn't getting anywhere.

"Well, how about Colonel Griffith? Can you put me through to him?"

"One moment."

After that moment, Colonel Griffith came on the line. "Yes, Jake?"

"Hi, Bill. Listen, we have a problem here."

"Right, you're missing a daughter. I guess there's been some kind of routing change that I didn't know about."

"Oh, so that's it."

"Lila's on the wrong plane, and I'm doing some follow-up now to find out where it went. It shouldn't take too long."

"How soon before I find out?"

"I'll call you."

"All right."

"Good-bye."

Click. Griffith hung up—rather abruptly, Dr. Cooper thought. As a matter of fact, Griffith didn't sound like himself through the whole conversation. He didn't apologize for the mix-up, and something like this would usually upset Bill Griffith very much. Besides that, Dr. Cooper got the impression that his friend didn't really want to talk to him at all, but just wanted to get the phone call over with.

Dr. Cooper figured he'd wait there in the room—prepare for tomorrow's lecture and see if a telephone call would come. But he was determined he would not wait for very long.

Cold. All around, nothing but cold and dark and beads of wetness against ringing metal. The earth was moving, shifting, swaying like a small boat on the sea.

Lila opened her eyes, but no light met them. She closed them again, this time in pain. Her head was throbbing, and her stomach was queasy. She heard no sounds at all until she began to stir, and then she could hear only the sound of her clothing, her shoes, her fingers passing over the cold metal shell that surrounded her. Her hand went to her head and found a bump. It could have been bleeding, but there was no way to tell in the dark and the wetness.

After just a short moment to let her head clear, she

raised her head and opened her eyes again. There was nothing to see but total blackness. Then she began to remember: the weapons pod, that big canister she'd crawled into. She was still inside it, but . . . something wasn't right. She doubted very much that there was still a solid, flying airplane outside that hatch.

She recalled the sounds she'd heard—the explosion, the ripping metal, the sudden gushing of water.

She dwelt on one thought longer than any other: *I'm alive. Lord God, how did You do it? I'm alive!*

She sat up very carefully, feeling above her head to make sure she wouldn't bang it again. The act of sitting up made her head swim, and she thought she would throw up.

*Easy, girl, take it slow. Breathe a little while.*

The thought of breathing made her think of that oxygen bottle she'd been using. She leaned close to the floor and felt around. Her hand found it, and she pressed the mask to her face. Ah, that felt much better. The sound of her breathing echoed around inside the pod as if she were in a huge tin can. She remained still and kept breathing from the mask until her stomach settled down and her head was clear again.

Then she began to explore the immediate area with her hands, trying to recall what little she was able to see before the hatch was sealed shut. Her hand found a cold, steal rib. She felt its curving shape and remembered that the pod was cylindrical, like a huge bottle. Evidently the pod wasn't level now, but was slanting uphill. She edged her way down the sloping floor, finding a few packages and tools scattered around, and finally found the hatch at the lower end.

She called out, "Hello!" but there was no response. She called a few more times, but the loud echo of her voice inside the metal bell only hurt her ears, and no one answered.

Her hand found a canvas bag nearby, and before

long she was able to locate a zipper and open it. Inside she could feel some cold, steel tools. Yes, this was a hammer . . . and this was a wrench . . . here were some screwdrivers . . . pliers . . . Oh! A flashlight!

She found the button and clicked it on. The light stung her eyes at first, but she was very glad to have a view of her world inside this big bottle.

Yes, she could see that the pod had taken quite a tumble. Except for one very large crate that was strapped down, bags, boxes, and small items were scattered everywhere. The walls were cold and damp with condensation. She judged that the weapons pod had to be about twenty-five feet in length and about six feet wide. It had a flat floor, but the walls and ceiling were one curved surface.

She noticed blood on her hand. She touched the bump on her head and found even more blood on her hand.

There had to be something in here to put on the wound, some cloth or bandage or something. She started crawling up the slanting floor toward the upper end, looking here and there for any box that might be a first aid kit.

She got a little past the middle of the pod and stopped short. The pod was swaying a little. She could make it move just by shifting her weight.

She had to be floating in the ocean . . . or under the ocean, or maybe half in the water and half out, or . . .

She didn't really know *where* she was.

Dr. Cooper and Jay slept through the night and were not awakened by the ring of the telephone. By midmorning, there still had been no word. Dr. Cooper called the hotel desk to see if there were any messages—there were none. He called Yokota Air Base, but no one knew anything and Colonel Griffith was unavailable.

They went downstairs to the hotel's restaurant for some breakfast, and it was there that a waiter brought them a written message: "Hoshi Park, noon—Griffith."

Nearby Hoshi Park was one huge Japanese garden, a very peaceful, very beautiful spot with closely manicured lawns, winding paths, and majestic trees forming whispering canopies. Every sculptured shrub, every reflective pond, every garden pagoda was perfectly placed, creating a rare place of rest and serenity. It was a favorite place for people to relax, to go for walks, to unwind.

Dr. Cooper and Jay appreciated the beauty all around them, but as they walked down one narrow path along a deep, glassy pond, their minds were only on Lila, their eyes were only looking for Colonel William Griffith.

Suddenly, almost sneakily, *he* found *them*. Griffith stepped onto the path abruptly from behind some trees, wearing civilian clothes.

"Hi," he said quietly. "Come with me."

They followed him down a small side-path, and he led them to a small grotto and waterfall where there were some benches. He sat down, and they joined him.

"Sorry for the secretive methods here," he said in a lowered voice. "I'm not supposed to be talking to you."

"I wish you would," said Dr. Cooper.

"Well, this may be the only chance I'll get. I'm due back at the base in less than an hour. Things are heating up over there. There's been a major development." He looked at them both as he sorted through what words to use. "All right . . . To begin with, what I told you about Lila being on the wrong flight was a lie. There were some other people standing nearby who could hear what I said, and our orders were clear: you weren't supposed to know anything about the fate of the plane."

"The fate of the plane?" Jay asked with alarm.

"Let's have it," said Dr. Cooper calmly but with concern.

"The plane is missing." Griffith added quickly, "But that doesn't mean it has crashed. We're following standard search and rescue procedures at the present time, but we really don't know for sure what happened."

Dr. Cooper put his hand on Griffith's arm and asked clearly and slowly, "Bill, what do you know? Be silent if you have to, but don't lie to us."

William Griffith could see the earnestness in Dr. Cooper's eyes. "Jake, it's because of our friendship and my love for you and your family that I'm breaking security and talking to you at all. Now there are some things I cannot tell you, but what I do tell you, you must promise me you'll hold in strict confidence."

Dr. Cooper and Jay both nodded. They were very concerned and listened intently.

"MAC 50231 was heading for the States and was on course for several hours, but then it became overdue in calling in a position report. Honolulu couldn't raise them, and neither could San Francisco or a commercial airliner. The last reported position of the plane was in the North Pacific, about halfway between Japan and the Aleutians. There are Search and Rescue planes combing that area now, but we haven't heard anything."

"The North Pacific . . ." said Dr. Cooper quietly, his face pale.

Griffith drew a breath and continued, his voice even lower, "But there's more to this than anyone's telling. I've been able to intercept some Intelligence reports that they're reexamining the last position report picked up by the control center in Tokyo. It seems they've decided not to trust it."

Jay guessed, "So . . . maybe the position reports were *false?*"

"No one is saying so, but I think there's a strong

possibility, especially since I learned some other bits of information. First of all, Anderson Air Force Base in Guam did pick up an unidentified blip on their radar at about 3 A.M. Greenwich Time, which would be about 1 in the afternoon for Guam. And if you figure the time it would have taken for the Starlifter to change course from its northern route, fly south, and come within range of Guam's radar, that would put it there at about that time. Secondly, it wasn't long afterwards that a Mayday distress signal went out from that location. Add to that a very short, garbled, identification signal that Guam picked up that could have been the identification code for 50231."

"So . . . the plane headed *south* instead of east?" asked Dr. Cooper.

Griffith nodded.

"But . . . how can you be sure?"

"I'm not. But somebody's sure enough to be sending some high security investigation teams down to the Carolines, and there's been some mention of using SR-71 reconnaissance planes. They have to be awfully sure to be sending all that manpower and gear down there."

"So why haven't they told us?" asked Dr. Cooper with anger in his voice.

"Jake, they aren't about to tell you anything, even if it is your daughter on that plane. The flight was carrying classified cargo of a very sensitive nature; so there's a strong possibility that the plane was hijacked. That means international complications, and that means they're going to handle it themselves, their way, and they won't want you involved."

"And you expect us to just sit and let them do whatever they want, whenever and however they want, while Lila's life may be in jeopardy?"

Griffith smiled a faint, knowing smile. "No. Not at all, Jake Cooper. I know good and well you're going to get involved, one way or another, no matter what anyone tells you. So let me help you."

"How?"

"All I can do is steer you in the right direction, give you a contact, and then . . . you're on your own. Listen, there is some kind of political trouble developing down in those islands—Communists, of course, perhaps Philippine guerrillas. It's a long shot, a flimsy theory at best, but this whole plane disappearance could be related to certain undesirable people down there wanting to get their hands on whatever was aboard that plane."

"So where do we even start to look for it?"

"I've already sent a telegram to someone I know on Pulosape."

*"Where?"* asked Jay.

Griffith only raised his eyebrows and gave a slight shrug. "An island in the Caroline group. You'd need a very large map to find it."

"Go on," said Dr. Cooper.

"She's a writer and journalist. She's been getting some tips about some kind of Communist activity in that island group, and she's been snooping around down there for a while. She's a very inquisitive sort, and if anything's cooking or if anything unusual has happened, there's a good chance she'll know about it. I should be hearing back from her any time."

"Well, who is she? Is she reliable?"

"Quite reliable. I've always known her to get whatever she's after, and she comes through for her friends."

"How can we reach her?"

"Can't wait, huh?" Griffith reached into his shirt pocket and pulled out a piece of paper, handing it to Dr. Cooper. "You won't be able to reach her by phone, but here's her name and the trade store on Pulosape where you can leave a radio message."

Dr. Cooper read the name on the paper. "Meaghan Flaherty."

"Ever met her?"

Dr. Cooper strained to remember. "I've probably

seen her name in print, but . . . I don't remember meeting her."

"Well, believe me, if you ever did meet her you'd remember, all right."

# FOUR

Pulosape was nothing more than a small volcanic mound of black rock and thick vegetation in the vast blue table of the South Pacific, a small, thirty-mile-long island that served no other real purpose than to be a stopping and resting point for passing fishing boats, trade schooners, and yachtsmen who were lost.

On the lee side of the island, serving as the very center of the island's activity and culture, was Bad Dave's Trade Store, a miserable, gloomy box with concrete walls cracked by too many earthquakes and a tin roof weighed down with old tires to keep the next hurricane from blowing it away. Parked in the deeply rutted road in front was Bad Dave's coconut-battered Land Rover, and only a hundred feet down a shallow bank were the crashing and hissing waves of the Pacific.

Inside the store, local natives wearing grass skirts and little else browsed and handled their way up and down the crowded shelves of clothing, tools, fuel cans, vegetables, and hog carcasses. Sailors, fishermen, and travelers looked for obscure repair parts, lengths of rope, fishhooks.

Bad Dave kept busy at the counter, bartering, arguing, selling, bellowing, and swapping the latest news, no matter how stretched the tales might be.

He was a big, sun-tanned man built like a tank, who always had a wad of gum in his mouth and a roll of very wrinkled dollar bills in his shirt pocket. He'd been living on this island and practically running it single-handedly for twenty-six years. He knew almost everyone who came sailing through, knew whom he liked and whom he didn't, who owed him money from their last time in the store and how much.

He was having a good time today and was not at all ready for the interruption when Bojo, his hired native, stepped quickly out of a back room, hurried behind the counter, and whispered something in his ear.

"You sure?" Dave whispered back.

Bojo nodded. "Bad! Big, black! Hungry!"

"Who else is back there?"

"Only two," said Bojo. "Red Hair and Kelly."

Dave winced. "Kelly. Bojo, we'll keep this to ourselves, all right?"

Bojo nodded, following Dave to the back room. Dave grasped the handle on the door and opened it very slowly.

Within the room, surrounded on every side by heavily stocked shelves of canned goods, dried goods, and machinery parts, two people sat at a small table opposite each other, a well-used chessboard between them.

One was Kelly, a stubborn little sailor who managed to keep himself idle for most of his years, and who had a very risky passion for betting—on *anything*.

The other was a flower, a crimson-crowned jewel, a heaven-sent angel that had floated in on a cloud of blessing. That was how Bad Dave liked to describe the woman sitting at the chess table, presently engaging Kelly in a steely-eyed stare-down that had to have been going on for hours.

Her name was Meaghan Flaherty, a writer. She was casually dressed in light slacks and a work shirt, and her red hair cascaded over her shoulders like surf over the rocks at sunset.

But right now she was more a marble statue than a woman. She was frozen, unmoving, unwavering, unblinking.

Dave looked at Kelly. The little sailor was frozen as well, although one eye twitched just a bit.

Dave leaned over and whispered to Bojo, "How long have they been at it?"

"An hour, maybe. They were playing chess for a bet, but then Red Hair made the bet bigger. She said, 'Kelly, how long can you sit there and not move a muscle?' And he said, 'Forever, ma'am.' And she said, 'Would you like to bet on that?' And he said, 'You have a bet,' and so . . ."

"So they've been sitting there like that for all this time?"

Bojo nodded.

Dave shook his head. "Sun's going down. It won't warm up in here 'til morning."

"They will not make it."

"I know Kelly won't. Mrs. Flaherty . . . eh, she always has surprised me."

"So . . . what can we do?"

"Wait, that's all. We'll close the place early and keep the doors shut. Nobody gets in, understand? Try to keep it quiet around here. I'll keep watch over them for now. You come to take your turn about 10 tonight."

Bojo left the room and found a place to sleep atop some grass mats. Dave stayed in the back room, supposedly refereeing the great wager, but spending most of the time with his eyes on the lady's pant leg and his hand very near the handle of a razor-sharp machete.

The hours passed. Midnight came. Kelly almost sneezed once, but managed to stifle it. Neither party moved. Now Bojo was taking his turn keeping watch, and just thinking of the pain those two must be feeling made his own muscles ache.

About 2 in the morning, Dave came into the room very quietly, carrying a kerosene heater. When Bojo saw what it was, he nodded as if to say, "Good idea."

Dave set the heater down very quietly near the chess table and spoke to the two human statues. "Thought maybe you could use a little heat. It's getting a little cool in here."

He lit the heater and stepped back quietly.

The room began to warm up, and within an hour the room was stifling. The betters' faces began to glisten and drip with sweat. Kelly was getting very glassy-eyed.

Now both Dave and Bojo were watching the lady's pant leg. With the heater so close to that leg, the heat had to be very uncomfortable.

Suddenly Bojo's eyes got wide, and he made just a slight noise that he stifled with his hand.

Dave held him still and whispered, "Not now, Bojo. Of all times, no noise now."

They could both see the pant leg stirring as if alive, heaving in and out, the wrinkles forming and then flattening.

Dave moved his hand very slowly toward the machete. The two sitting at the table didn't notice what he was doing. They were still staring at each other in total concentration.

The pant leg was still moving. Now they could see a bump moving down toward the cuff.

A shiny, black head suddenly emerged, weaving to and fro, a thin, red tongue licking the air.

Bojo clasped his hands together tightly to keep them from shaking. Dave gripped the machete.

The head dropped slowly to the wooden floor, dangling from a long, black, sleek body. The snake continued to pour inch by inch from the pant leg, slithering out from under the table and slowly exploring the room with wags of its black head and flickers of its red tongue.

It approached Dave, but he did not move until the right moment.

WHAM! The machete came down and instantly separated the snake's head from its body. The body curled and writhed and then lay still. The head came to rest with the white mouth gaping, the glistening fangs extended.

Bojo screamed simply because he had to.

Kelly lost the bet as he stole a glance sideways, saw the snake, and leaped out of his chair with a loud gasp and very salty language.

The lady expelled a long-held breath and relaxed, her head flopping forward.

"The Lord be praised," she said quietly. Then, with a trembling hand, she picked up her queen and gently bumped Kelly's king off the chessboard. "Checkmate."

Kelly only stood there, frozen with terror at the snake and unbelief at the lady's last move. "What . . . how can you . . . ?"

"I had all night to think about it," she said, wiping the sweat from her brow. Then she asked Dave, "Could you show a lady to the powder room?"

"Straight through there," said Dave, pointing.

She hurried out of the room as Kelly looked at the dead snake, then the chessboard, then Dave and Bojo.

"Sorry about this," Dave said. "We figure some of these devils must have come on the island with a load of bananas." He reached down and gathered up the dead snake, whistling his amazement at its size. "They like to crawl into warm, dark places at night to keep warm." He noticed a hole in the floor right under the chess table. "There's how he got in. Bojo, we'll have to patch that up."

Bojo nodded his head.

Kelly's face was full of questions, but he was still too terrified to say a word.

Dave told him, "It's a good thing you took up Mrs. Flaherty's bet. The snake was coiled around her leg. They say the bite only takes seconds to kill you. She saved both your skins."

Mrs. Flaherty returned, cooler and calmer. "Thank you, David."

Dave was turning off the kerosene heater. "You're very welcome, Mrs. Flaherty. I guess he finally got warm enough to want to leave your pant leg."

Kelly stared at the lady for a long time. She responded with a very relieved smile.

Kelly stammered, "You . . . you are quite a woman, Mrs. Flaherty."

She replied, "And you are a very worthy opponent, Mr. Kelly. But tell me, will you honor our agreement?"

"Huh?"

"I've won the chess game fair and square, and our bet too. Will you tell me what I want to know?"

Kelly still wasn't thinking straight and didn't answer.

Dave decided to help him. "C'mon, Kelly, you remember. You and those Commies were in cahoots, and everybody knows it."

Kelly brightened as if his memory had just clicked on, and said, "Oh, that." He looked at Mrs. Flaherty. "What was it you were asking me?"

Mrs. Flaherty motioned Kelly to a chair and took one herself. "When I first set foot on Pulosape, this island was crawling with Philippine guerrillas. You'd think they'd called a convention."

Dave grabbed an empty wooden barrel and sat down himself. "They were in the store all the time, with lots of money to spend and feeling pretty cocky. *Somebody's* been paying them in money and weapons, and they have some big caper going on *somewhere*."

Kelly forced a chuckle. "Heh. What would I know about that?"

Mrs. Flaherty was unbending. "They're gone now, and very suddenly, and I know it was you who ferried them away in your boat. Where did you take them, and why?"

Dave leaned in close. "A bet's a bet, and you've lost, remember that."

Kelly thought about that for a moment, and then nodded regretfully. "You can't tell them you got any of this from me."

"Agreed," said Mrs. Flaherty.

Kelly probed his mind for a starting-point. "There's about a hundred of them, all from the Philippines, a long way from home. They're being paid very well to carry out some special errand for their . . . their financiers."

"The Soviets?" asked Dave.

"Heh. Yeah, yeah, who else? Call it a fund-raiser. If they ever expect to overthrow the Philippines they have to have money, and the Soviets have struck a deal with them, paying them a *lot* to carry out some special business."

"What business?" asked Mrs. Flaherty.

"That I don't know, really. They wouldn't tell me. They just paid me to take them to Kurnoe and not ask questions, so I did."

"Kurnoe?"

"Eh, it's a little island north of here. Nobody there as far as I know . . . heh, except guerrillas. But something's supposed to happen up there really soon, and they're all getting ready for it."

"Can you show me how to get there?"

Kelly's eyes widened a little. "Hey, Mrs. Flaherty, you'd better learn how much is enough. You're only one little woman, and these guys are a hundred and *very* mean!"

Dave just shook his head and said, "Give the lady

what she wants, Kelly, unless you want to lock horns with her again for the rest of the night."

Kelly shrugged. "You've got charts, Dave. Get them out and I'll show you where it is. But, ma'am, you'll have to get there by yourself. I don't want those cut-throats seeing *me* bringing you into their plans."

"Fine," said Mrs. Flaherty. "Dave, I need to make a call to my Air Force chum in Japan."

"I'll warm up the radio," Dave answered.

Lila had taken a large canvas from the big crate inside the pod and had wrapped it several times around her for warmth. Now she sat in the pod in the dark, the flashlight turned off to save the batteries. She breathed from the oxygen bottle only now and then, trying to save that supply as well. She was trying to think, trying to pray.

"Lord," she prayed, "I don't know where I am or if I'll ever get out of here. Please help me. Please send someone to rescue me. Please . . ."

She stopped. She could feel the Lord speaking back to her, but what He was saying to her heart was not what she wanted to hear.

"Lord God, I need *help!* I can't think about that now!"

His still, small voice would not be silent. He was bringing a Scripture to her mind: "If you are present-ing your offering at the altar, and there remember that your brother has something against you, leave your offering there before the altar, and go your way; first be reconciled to your brother, and then come and pre-sent your offering."

Now she sat there in the dark not saying anything, not praying anything. *It's Dad's fault,* she thought. *It's always been his fault.*

"Lord," she said softly, a little afraid to say it, "You're not being fair. I was hurting already, and now You've dumped me into this mess."

She remembered some of her father's words shortly before she left Japan: "Lila, you have to think of others. The whole universe doesn't revolve around just *you.*"

"He should talk," she replied to her own thoughts. "Since when has he really cared about how *I* feel?"

But the Lord spoke to her heart again, and she argued with Him. "Lord . . . of *course* I'm thinking about myself! *I'm* the one in trouble right now! *I'm* the one who's hurting. *I'm* the one who just might die in here!"

*I, I, I.* It seemed like the Lord was pointing out to her how often she said that word.

"All right," she finally said reluctantly. "I'll . . . I'll talk about Dad, and Jay. I wonder what they're doing right now when I'm not with them? I wonder if they miss me?" A more sobering thought came to her. "I wonder if they even know I'm in trouble?"

The Lord spoke again. *Lila, now you're not only thinking about just yourself—you're also thinking about others thinking about you.*

She sagged with frustration and rested her head against the cold metal wall. "All right, all right. I'm thinking of myself."

*What about that time at the Air Base?*

"I was thinking of myself then, too. I never should have said what I said."

She could see the scene unfolding in her mind like a taped replay. She could see her father carrying her luggage toward the boarding gate. She could see the pain in his eyes.

She could recall him saying, "We'll talk about it."

And she could hear herself snipping back at him, "I'll believe that when I see it. You just don't care. You've never cared!"

And she could tell she'd hurt him; she'd scored a direct hit.

Lila erased the scene from her mind with a wag of

her head. "I didn't feel bad about saying it then . . . but I thought we'd be able to talk about it more. I thought I'd see him again." She could feel sorrow and despair creeping into her heart like bad news. "Lord, what if I die in here?"

The Lord seemed to be silent now. She felt no words from Him. But she knew what He was doing.

He was giving her time to think about it.

# FIVE

As Bad Dave's thirty-foot sloop moved through the reefs, Dave, Dr. Cooper, and Jay could see that the remote island of Kurnoe certainly held little that would interest any visitors. The island was small and flat, and except for an even carpeting of coconut-laden palm trees, it was featureless. Dave knew how to find the village on the lee side of the island, and now they had it in sight, a tiny and unimpressive cluster of grass huts and one very ugly structure constructed of rusting, corrugated metal and pieces of World War II airplanes. One wall was mostly the wing from a Japanese Zero, the emblem of the Rising Sun plainly visible.

Dave explained, "The only people ever interested in this little island were the Japanese, during the war. I've heard they used to have a secret airstrip on this little lump."

Dr. Cooper was looking at the village through binoculars. "An airstrip, eh? Big enough to land a Starlifter?"

"*If* it's really there in the first place, and *if* you had the manpower to repair and lengthen it."

"Oh . . . I would say they have all the men they need."

Dave nodded grimly. "Kelly was telling the truth. The Commies are here, all right, and probably aren't too happy to see us."

51

Dr. Cooper handed the binoculars to Jay, who took a look. He could see that many heavily armed, rough-looking characters were already gathering at the crude dock in front of the village, staring at the strange boat approaching.

"Just how are we supposed to get through that bunch?" Jay asked.

"I'm wondering how Mrs. Flaherty got through them," said Dr. Cooper.

Dave only shook his head. "Well, I told her not to set out alone, but she was afraid of losing their trail if she waited for you two. But she has her tricks. You'll see."

"What's *our* trick?" Jay asked.

"Eh, no problem. You're Christians, you know the Bible and how to act religious. We'll just tell them you're friends of Reverend Garrison, the missionary. Hopefully, by the time they ask you, Garrison will have gotten there to introduce himself, and you'll be telling the truth."

Dave eased back on the throttle and let the sloop ease gently toward the dock. A dozen Communist rebels, dressed in dull, camouflage fatigues and carrying machine guns, were on the dock. Only one caught the rope and helped to pull the boat alongside. The other eleven only stared at the arrivals and held their machine guns ready. Dave waved and smiled at the guerrillas, so Dr. Cooper and Jay did the same.

Dave said in a lowered voice, "I know the commander. Let me do the talking."

He stepped onto the dock to have a few words with the first man he encountered, a dark, very muscular man dressed in khaki, a large rifle slung on his back. Dave rattled off a quick, overly-friendly explanation in a Filipino dialect while the rebel leader studied Dr. Cooper and Jay for a very long, very scary moment.

The man was apparently spouting some protests

and angry questions, and Dave tried to answer them. The man laughed a cruel, conniving laugh and gave Dave a taunting shove. Dave tried to explain some more, but the rebel was through talking.

Whatever Dave had said, the rebel didn't buy it. He growled some orders to his men, and every gun suddenly pointed right at the three intruders.

Dave put his hands up and interpreted what the man was angrily yelling at them. "Uh . . . better put your hands up, and he wants you to get out of the boat, right *now!*"

Dr. Cooper looked at Jay as they both raised their hands. "So much for tricks."

They slowly started to climb out of the boat. These Communists were a rough bunch. They even *smelled* rough.

Just then a voice shouted from the land, "Randy! Jack! Praise God, what a surprise!"

Every eye turned toward the shore to see a jolly, deeply tanned, chubby man in a pair of faded beach pants trotting down the dock toward them, arms outstretched, his wide smile shining in the sun. Right behind him were two natives in woven grass skirts, also smiling broadly and chattering away in their own language. The guerrillas began to lose some of their fierceness. Several gun barrels sank slowly. Some of the men even seemed disappointed.

Dave shouted happily, spreading his arms for a hug. "Well, Jerry, long time no see!"

Dave and the chubby fellow collided in an embrace, patted each other's back, and had some good, loud laughs.

"Jerry!" Dr. Cooper shouted with a smile, extending his hand.

"Yeah, Jerry!" Jay shouted too, figuring it was the best thing to do.

Jerry reached down to them and gave them a very

strong helping hand out of the boat and onto the dock.

"So, how are things?" Jerry asked.

"Oh, fine, just fine," said Dr. Cooper.

"And Mary?"

"She's fine too."

"Well, say, I thought you'd never get here. Listen, I've got your room all set up in the church. Come on and I'll get you settled. Any luggage?"

"Well—"

"Moki, Sulu!" Jerry called to his two native accomplices, and then chattered some orders to them. They leaped into the boat and picked up the Coopers' gear. "Come on, let's have lunch!"

With that, the chubby man took the lead and began clearing a path through the guerrillas and guns. The three visitors followed him off the dock, followed in turn by the gear-toting natives.

"Keep laughing," Jerry told them quietly.

So they kept laughing, talking, pointing at things, making up names, doing anything they could think of to look like old chums, and kept it up until they had gotten deeper into the forest and out of sight.

"This way," said Jerry, leading them down a path through the palm trees.

After going just a short distance, they came to a small structure without walls, nothing more than a grass roof set on poles. Underneath the roof were some crude log benches arranged like church pews, and in front, a simple pulpit.

"Welcome to Kurnoe Congregational, the gospel outpost of the South Seas!" said Jerry. Then he extended his hand for real and said, "Jerry Garrison. What are your real names, Randy and Jack?"

"Dr. Jake Cooper."

"And I'm Jay."

"And I hope you know a Mary . . ."

Dr. Cooper smiled. "Well, I do have a cousin named Mary, and as far as I know, she really is fine."

"Good enough. I probably shouldn't have used deception just now, but . . . Anyway, you can see you've come at a bad time. I don't know if you're looking for trouble, but we have plenty right now."

"They're looking for a missing plane," said Dave. "Dr. Cooper's daughter is on board."

Jerry's eyes widened. "Oho! Is that so?" He nodded to himself, thought a few thoughts, and then said in a hushed voice, "These Commies have been here for a month or so, working on a deserted Japanese airstrip on the other side of the island."

Dr. Cooper and Jay exchanged excited glances.

"Praise God," said Dr. Cooper. "Looks like we're on the right track."

But Jerry wasn't smiling yet. "Oh, but you'd better be careful before you take one step, sir. These guerrillas mean business, and they are not kind to anyone they don't trust. You saw the murder in their faces." Jerry stepped just a little closer to mutter the next piece of information. "And I think things are worse now. They haven't said anything to me, but from the way they act and talk, I'm sure something's gone wrong. Their plan isn't working out."

"What do you mean?"

"Three days ago, they all went to the other side of the island, to the airstrip, and waited, but nothing happened, and no airplane came. Ever since then, they've been very agitated and suspicious, with boats and men coming and going, and show no mercy on strangers with no good reason to be here. I'm very glad I saw your boat land and got out there in time. You could have been shot right there, you know."

"Why weren't we?" asked Dave.

Jerry smiled. "Mmm, I've been good to the guerrillas. I've fed them, showed them hospitality. Usually they permit friends of mine to go on living. Just like that other visitor, that lady . . ."

Dave knew who that was. "Meaghan Flaherty!"

But Jerry only gave Dave a funny look. "Who?"

"A very lovely woman, long, shimmering, red hair, about this tall . . ."

Jerry only shook his head. "No, heavens no. You think a beautiful woman would last more than one hour among this terrible bunch? No, this was a cloth trader, an old woman from one of the southern islands. I convinced the guerrillas that they could use some material to patch their clothes and such, so they let her come ashore to do business."

Now Dave was giving Jerry a funny look. "Uh . . . just where might we find this woman?"

"Oh, I imagine she'd be down at the trade store. You know, that old shack made out of Japanese airplane scraps."

The island's trade store, just like Bad Dave's back on Pulosape, was the center of island commerce—the little, scrap metal building where goods and supplies were bought and sold, stories were swapped, drinks were served. It was a tight, smelly little place that had been washed away a few times by tidal waves, but pieced together again out of whatever debris happened to float along—in this case, leftover airplane parts.

At the moment, the place was packed with idle, Communist rebels, all facing toward the center of the room where a table—made from an airplane's tail—had been set up. Two people sat at the table opposite each other: a strong, handsome native with muscular body and dark skin, and an old native woman, the cloth trader, heavyset, gray, dressed in all manner of brightly colored materials as an advertisement of her wares.

On the table between the two was a small pile of coins and a gold locket on a chain. In front of each person was a tin plate.

On each tin plate was a heaving, oozing, crawling mass of very large snails, crawling over and around each other, their antennae weaving and probing about. Several empty shells on each plate showed that many snails had already disappeared. A bet was clearly on.

The man reached for a snail, tugged it from the tin plate, held the shell in his hand, and then dug the snail out with a small fork. With a very cocky expression, he threw back his head and dropped the snail into his mouth, swallowing it whole. He washed it down with a small glass of liquor.

Now all eyes were on the old woman. The whole place was murmuring with anticipation.

She smiled a jagged, toothy smile and did the same thing, dropping a snail into her mouth and swallowing it. She washed it down with a small glass of water.

Now all eyes were on the man, wondering what he would do. He looked just a little sick, but he kept forcing a sly smile anyway, and this time he dug out *two* snails and swallowed both of them at once, following that with another gulp of liquor.

All eyes shifted to the woman. She pondered her next move for just a moment, then smiled her toothy grin, cackled a little, and dug out *four* snails, chomping them down and downing another glass of water.

There was a roar of anticipation this time as all eyes turned to the man. Could he match that? Would he try to top it?

He took a deep breath, stretched his body to ease the pressure on his swelling belly, and then . . . reached for *six* snails as the crowd went wild with hoots and laughter. Into his mouth they went—one, two, three, four, five, six. His cheeks were puffed out as he chomped on the slimy mass. He swallowed several times and then grabbed desperately for another glass of liquor.

The old woman pondered her next move, but she also had an eye on her opponent. He did seem to be weaving a bit. He was holding his mouth shut very tightly as if expecting an explosion of some kind. She smiled her toothy smile, let out a cry of glee, and began to dig out six . . . then seven . . . and then *eight* snails, lifting each one up for the man to see. He watched her prepare each and every snail, one by one, his eyes getting glassy, his face turning quite pale.

With all eight snails ready in her hand, she threw her head back, lifted the snails high over her mouth, and . . .

The man suddenly clapped his hand over his mouth and ran from the room. The guerrillas roared and cheered. The old lady dropped the eight snails back onto the tin plate and smiled a smile of obvious relief, shoving the plate aside. Someone took the snails away. The bet was over.

She reached for the coins and the locket, dropped them into a little pouch, and rose to leave as the crowd continued to cheer and pay off some of the bets they had made with each other. Many had bet on the woman, and they were hilarious in victory. Some had bet on the man, and most of them were good sports about it.

One man, however, had lost his bet and didn't feel good about it at all. As the old woman made her way to the door, he stood in her path, very tall, very mean. Two other men joined him, one on each side, and together they formed a very ugly wall.

The woman stopped and looked up at them, her face full of questions.

The man put out his hand. He wanted that little pouch. His two friends were hitting their palms with their fists, a very threatening gesture.

"Hey, what do you know?" came a voice behind them.

The three roughnecks were startled and turned to see who it was. Two men and a lad were standing in the doorway.

The old woman didn't hesitate, but tossed the pouch to the man in the middle.

That man happened to be Jake Cooper.

"Look out, man!" hollered Bad Dave as the three rebels came at them.

Bad Dave planted his fist squarely on the jaw of the man on the left. Dr. Cooper was able to flip the middle one aside. Jay dove between the legs of the third assailant and came up on the other side just in time to catch the pouch, tossed to him by his father.

Two more rebels came at Jay, so he dove under a table and then wriggled across the floor just out of their reach. One rebel almost grabbed his heel, but the old woman managed to stick her leg out just in time to trip him. His head met the edge of the table with a crunch, and he became just another rug on the floor.

Jay was about to be sacked by a towering wave of Communists, but he saw the old woman in the clear and hit her with a short pass. The first man who came after her got his eyes poked, so he stumbled about, getting in the way of the others. That gave the woman just enough time to toss the pouch back to Dr. Cooper.

Intercepted! A lanky, dirty rebel snatched the pouch out of the air with a cry of victory and held it aloft for the others to see.

And then it was out of his hand, snatched away by Jay, who immediately turned to run. The rebel grabbed Jay around the middle and lifted him up, but that only gave Jay the perfect opportunity to kick another man's face and send him sprawling. As for the rebel holding him, both his arms were occupied, so he could do nothing to prevent the old woman from shattering a bottle on his head. He let go of Jay on his way to the floor, and Jay tossed the pouch to Dr. Cooper again, which meant Dr. Cooper had to immediately stoop to let a rebel flop over him and then spring upward to send the rebel flying over the bar. A kick from Dr. Cooper's boot took care of a second attacker, just in time for the old woman to slip by on her way to the door. Dr. Cooper handed off the pouch to her, and she dashed out the door with another guerrilla right behind her.

Suddenly the door closed and the guerrilla's face came to a sudden stop against it. He tumbled backward to the floor.

"Ohhhhh," said the old woman in mock pity, peeking around the door.

Some guns were coming out now. The game was getting very dangerous.

But Bad Dave called a halt to everything with one simple act.

"Hey, everybody!" he shouted, and it was amazing how fast he got everyone's attention.

Maybe it was because he held a stick of dynamite in his hand, the fuse lit and burning.

Everyone in the room instantly became a statue. Then, after only a split second, every opening in the building, even if it was a window, became a door. Guerrillas and natives alike were popping out of that little shack like cannon fire, scattering in all directions.

"Let's go," said Dave, holding the dynamite high over his head for all to see.

He bolted out the door, followed by the Coopers and the old woman, and everyone cleared the way for them with the utmost courtesy. They ran for the forest, heading back toward the church.

But Dr. Cooper could see that fuse getting very short. "Dave, drop that thing! You'll get us all killed!"

"Not until we're safe!"

"Safe?" yelled Jay. "I don't feel very safe right *now!*"

"Aw, you worry too much!"

They kept running until they came to the church. The fuse kept burning shorter and shorter. It was down to an inch now.

The Coopers dove into the brush, covering their heads.

Dave and the old woman just stood there, watching the fuse burn down.

Finally it did.

"Mm, not bad," said Dave, looking at the dead stick of dynamite.

The old woman spoke for the first time, and it was startling to hear the old Polynesian speaking with such a crisp, Irish accent. "Dave, one of these days you'll try this trick twice on the same bunch, and then where will you be?"

Dr. Cooper's head rose out of the grass, and then Jay's, and they looked back toward the trail where Dave and the woman stood. As they watched from a safe distance, Dave peeled the wrapping off the dynamite, and then peeled what it really was—a banana. He took a bite, then offered a bite to the woman. She reached into her mouth first and removed her jagged, false teeth so she could bite into it with her own.

Dave started laughing, his cheek full of banana. "Hey, come on, boys! Come share a banana with the jewel of the South Pacific and everywhere else too: Mrs. Meaghan Flaherty!"

Dr. Cooper and Jay looked at each other, and Dr. Cooper could only sigh.

"Son," he said, "we've been had."

As they came out of hiding, the old woman removed her gray wig and let a cascade of red locks fall.

She extended her hand. "Dr. Jacob Cooper. I've heard much about you and your children from our mutual friend, Colonel William Griffith."

He shook her hand, still amazed. "Pleased to meet you. This is my son, Jay."

She shook his hand as well. "A pleasure, Jay."

Dave handed her a damp cloth and she wiped the native darkness and the lines of age from her skin, revealing a fair complexion underneath.

Dave smiled, very proud of her. "I was wondering

how you figured you'd survive among that rowdy bunch."

"I almost didn't. It was going well for a time, but things were taking a nasty turn when you three showed up. I'm very grateful."

"But just what was that all about?" asked Dr. Cooper. "We had ourselves an all-out brawl back there and we could have been killed, and for what? A little pouch of money?"

She brought out the pouch. "No, not the money. I wouldn't swallow raw snails for any amount of that. But that man had a locket, and my eye caught the name on it. I thought you'd be interested."

She reached into the pouch and pulled out the locket. It was gold and delicate, a small heart on a chain. She turned it over and placed it in Dr. Cooper's hand.

Dr. Cooper recognized it immediately. Jay did too. They were both familiar with the inscription on the back:

"To my daughter Lila on her thirteenth birthday."

# SIX

Dr. Cooper and Jay could hardly contain their excitement and their curiosity.

"That man you were competing with in there . . ." said Dr. Cooper. "Where did he get this?"

Mrs. Flaherty shook her head. "He wouldn't tell me. He wouldn't say a word about it until I won it from him fair and square." She looked back toward the trade store. "And now, considering the party we just had in there, I don't think I'll go back to discuss it with him further."

"I can't believe God's providence! We're on the right trail, all right, but . . ."

Jay asked, "Did he give you any clues at all?"

"One clue," said Mrs. Flaherty. "He said he got it from an old pearl diver."

Dave muttered, "Aw, the islands are full of them. You can take your pick."

"Come on," said Dr. Cooper. "We'll see what Jerry the missionary knows."

Jerry was relieved to see them all safe, and very intrigued to see who the old cloth trading lady really was. They told him about the bet and the lively exchange that followed.

"You . . . you got into a *fight* with the rebels?" he asked in horror.

"Over this locket," said Dr. Cooper, showing it to Jerry. "It belongs to my daughter. We have to find out where that fellow got it."

Jerry's eyes were wide with fear. "More important than that, you need to get off this island. I know the rebel commander. He won't let you get away with what you did back there. You must leave at once!"

Dr. Cooper stuck to business. "The man said he got it from an old pearl diver. Would you have any guess who that might be?"

Jerry only had to think for a moment. "Kolo. It could be old Kolo, from Tukani. He's more of a scavenger than a pearl diver. He dives into old wrecks, sunken warplanes, you name it, collecting junk he thinks he can sell to souvenir hunters and such. He's not very respected and actually is very shiftless, but he's the one I would suspect, all right."

"Tukani?"

"It's not far from here. You could sail there by morning."

"That's our next stop, then. Dave, will you take us there?"

"Sure thing, Doc," said Dave.

"Wait!" said Jerry. "If you're going to Tukani, you'd better be warned about the people living there, the Sutolos!"

"Are they hostile?" asked Dr. Cooper.

"Well, they love visitors," said Jerry. "For *dinner,* that is. They're cannibals."

"Oh, great!" said Dave.

"Well, Dave," said Jerry, "I don't think you or Dr. Cooper have much to worry about—you'd be too old and tough. But young Jay, and Mrs. Flaherty . . . well . . ."

"We have Lila to think about," said Dr. Cooper. "Let's get going. Jerry, we'd like you to come along if you can."

"Oh, you go on ahead, and quickly! I'll stay here

and try to delay the rebels. Don't worry about me. I'll catch up. Dave, here's how to get to Tukani."

Jerry and Dave had a quick conference about navigation and compass headings, and then all but Jerry grabbed their belongings and slinked under the cover of the falling darkness toward the dock where Dave's boat was moored.

Several hours later, as darkness shrouded the island and all its inhabitants were settling in for the night, several dark figures stole through the forest around the little island church. They moved quickly, darting from tree to tree, hiding, sneaking, drawing ever closer to the little chapel. Only rarely could the glint of an eye or the bluish reflection from a gun barrel be seen in the moonlight.

Then the leaves of grass parted, and several pairs of glistening eyes peered into the church. They could see several cots set out, and the visitors sleeping on them— the two strange Americans, the longtime islander called Bad Dave, and the mysterious cloth lady who could outswallow anyone.

The first man to step out of hiding and into the church was the rebel commander, the gruff character who first met these strangers at the dock. His face was full of menace as he signaled the others to move in. They stepped very silently into the church, taking up positions all around the unsuspecting, sleeping visitors.

Then, with machine gun ready and pointing, the commander stepped over to Dr. Cooper's cot and clamped his hand around the archaeologist's neck.

Dr. Cooper's head rolled off the cot and onto the ground. It was nothing but a pillow wearing a hat.

The young lad was a log in a sleeping bag. The old lady was a pile of her cloth with no one inside. Bad Dave was a pile of grass.

The commander was enraged! With one quick command and a wave of his arm, he ran for the missionary's

66

hut with all his men following him, guns ready. They came to the little hut in the woods, kicked in the frail door, and found the missionary asleep in bed.

The darkness came alive with blazing rifle barrels spitting fire and lead, spraying the missionary's bed with enough gunfire to kill several men.

The commander threw back the blankets.

Jerry Garrison was another dummy made of straw.

The commander barked some more orders, and the band of killers stormed down to the dock. Bad Dave's boat was gone. The cloth lady's little boat was still there and was immediately sunk with a hail of gunfire. Then the rebel leader and his men gathered to lay their plans.

There was no night, no day, no way to tell how much time had passed in that cold, silent crypt. Lila had prayed until she'd run out of things to say, until her heart was empty, until her mind was exhausted. She'd slept for some time, an oxygen mask on her face so she wouldn't suffocate in her sleep.

When she awoke, nothing had changed. The nightmare was not over. The cold metal container still surrounded her; there still was no sound. But her mind was working again, and she was ready to try something as soon as she could figure out exactly what.

She sat there for a while, shining her flashlight and looking at the hatch. As far as she could tell, it was the only way in or out of this can. She had no idea what she would find on the other side, but there was only one way to find out. If she could just . . . *crack* it open, just a little. There had to be some way to open it.

She carefully checked the mechanism. The latch was on the outside, and there seemed to be no way to unlock the hatch from the inside. She began to examine the seams all around the hatch. They were sealed tight.

She pulled the bag of tools close, dug out a large screwdriver, and tried prying at the seam. She wasn't surprised to find that it wouldn't move at all. It was very strongly constructed and wasn't about to yield to a screwdriver in the hand of a thirteen-year-old.

*Well,* Lila thought, *I still don't know what all my options are. I don't know everything there is to know about this pod.*

She decided to find out. She knew what was in the cloth tool bag, so she pushed that aside. What else was in this tomb with her?

The most obvious thing was the very large, rectangular crate that took up most of the inside of the pod. She decided to learn about that first. She inched carefully uphill toward it, feeling the pod sway just a little with her movement, until she was close to the crate.

There were no obvious markings on the outside. It was just a plain wood box, the lid nailed shut. She inched her way all around it, carefully getting to know it, looking for any labels that would tell her anything, looking for any weak spots that might open easily. She found nothing.

She inched back down the pod and got her tool bag, then returned. The crowbar should work.

She jammed the tip of the crowbar into the crack under the lid and started prying. Ah, this lid was going to be more cooperative than the hatch. It began to come free without much trouble. She loosened one nail, then another, then another, working her way down one side of the crate, around the lower end, and then around the upper end. The lid was ready to lift back. With one strong but careful shove, she lifted it up and pushed it back to where it rested against the pod wall.

Whatever was inside was covered with styrofoam packing material. She dug the styrofoam aside.

What in the world was this? It looked like a prop

from a science fiction movie, something like a robot or a satellite. It had a long, cylindrical body of shining metal and glass, and then, sticking out one end, looking like a robot's head on the end of a narrow, rotating neck, was a periscope, or a camera, or some kind of weird device with one very large, deep, red lens that made it look like a one-eyed creature from another planet.

She dug aside more of the styrofoam. There were some thin, spidery arms further down, all folded up very tightly to fit into the crate, and . . . what was this? Some kind of metal cover, held on with simple screws.

She grabbed her screwdriver and started removing the screws. It was easy. She lifted the cover aside.

Ah. A control panel of some kind. Switches, buttons, digital displays, indicator lights. She studied it for a long time, trying to figure out just what this strange contraption was. Too bad it didn't come with a manual. Did it have an On-Off switch? What about this switch right here?

She flipped it on.

Three red lights blinked on, making her jump a little. But that was all. She flipped the switch off, and the lights disappeared. She flipped the switch on again, and the lights turned on. There was no sound, and nothing else happened. Well, that was something anyway. She turned off her flashlight and noticed that the red lights provided enough light to see, which would be useful.

Oh, here was another button marked "Activate." She thought carefully about pushing that one. How could she be sure what it would do?

Bracing herself, and leaning back a little, she pressed the button.

Nothing.

She relaxed and pushed it again, figuring that would turn off whatever she may have turned on.

Now . . . what did *this* lever do? It was just a little thing, only about two inches long, but it reminded her of the joysticks that come with computer games. She was pretty skillful with those; maybe she could make something work with this one. She tried it. Nothing happened.

Hmmm. She pressed the Activate button again. Then she moved the lever forward.

There was a whirring sound that made her jump. She let go of the lever, and the sound stopped. The sound had come from the robot-head. Ah! It had moved. The big red eye was looking just a little to the side now. She moved the lever again. The head turned some more, pivoting on the narrow neck, the eye looking sideways. She moved the lever the other way, and the head rotated back to where it had begun, the eye looking straight up.

*Well, Lila, you're making progress, at least with this machine.*

But after another half-hour of tinkering and experimenting, Lila called it quits. She could make the red lights come on, and she could rotate the head, but that was all, and it certainly wasn't helping her get out of there.

So she settled back to think some more. All that styrofoam packing could be useful. She found a bag of small parts and emptied it. Then she stuffed it full with the styrofoam to make a life preserver. She smiled. That was a good idea. Now she'd have some flotation when she got out of here.

But she still had to get out of here!

She looked at the hatch again. There was a large plate in the center, held on by a dozen bolts. Maybe the locking mechanism was behind it. Some wrenches in the tool bag might loosen the bolts, and then . . . well, it was worth trying.

She slid downhill to the hatch, bringing her tool

bag with her, and soon found a wrench that fit the bolts. She locked the wrench on the first bolt and pushed against the wrench with all her weight. The bolt started twisting out. With a few more forceful twists, the bolt began to turn very easily, and soon she had it out. One by one, she removed the bolts, dropping them into the tool bag for safekeeping.

The last bolt came out, and then she pried off the plate. Yes, there was some kind of mechanism inside, just like the workings of a door lock. She recognized a shaft that had to operate the latch. All she had to do was get it to turn.

She found another wrench to do the job and fit the jaws around the shaft. Then she got scared. *What if this thing bursts open?* She braced her body against the hatch and then, with a very careful, very slight motion, turned the shaft only a fraction.

The lock was working, all right.

"Lord . . . please protect me . . ." she prayed.

She had a thought and reached for her oxygen bottle, clipping it to her belt and putting the mask over her face.

She put her hands on the wrench again and turned the shaft another fraction of a turn. She checked the seams around the hatch. No sign of water, or leaks, or anything.

She turned the shaft just a little more. She thought she heard some bubbles escaping from somewhere. The sound stopped, though.

A little more. There. Now she could see a very small leak at the bottom of the hatch, nothing very big.

Just a little more . . .

The hatch suddenly exploded inward! It slammed her aside, throwing her against the pod wall. She hit her head against the metal, and everything went black for a moment. A wall of water was pouring in through the hatch!

She strained against the hatch, trying to swing it shut, but there was no holding back such a mighty flood of water.

The pod began to shift! This end was sliding, dropping! The weight of the water was rapidly pulling it down!

Lila was floating, trying desperately to grab something and so keep from being tossed around the pod by the swirling water.

Now the pod was sliding downhill. She could hear the scraping sound of rocks and sand moving across the bottom of the hull. It was moving faster, rocking, bouncing, rumbling along.

Lila grabbed the ribs of the pod and climbed upward, trying to get out of the rising water, hoping somehow to get to safety.

Suddenly the pod slammed into rocks and sand, coming to a crashing halt with a loud CHUNG! Lila was knocked back down into the swirling water where she was lost for a moment, completely submerged, reaching frantically for a handhold, not knowing which way was up.

When her head bobbed above the surface, she could see the red lights on the strange machine. She reached for the ribs of the pod again and moved toward the lights, climbing out of the water.

The pod had stopped moving and was now tilted very steeply. The big wooden crate was lashed down and so didn't move from its place. But some of the other objects in the pod had slid free and were now floating in the water that had filled the lower half. As for the tool bag, it was most likely at the very bottom of the pod, under the water. Lila found a place to perch atop one end of the big wooden crate, and took a moment to rest and think.

She noticed that her ears were hurting. The pressure in the pod had increased with the inflow of the water. No doubt it was the trapped air that had kept the water level down to where it was. But the increased pressure told her one thing for sure: she was under the ocean, perhaps quite deep, although how deep she couldn't be sure.

She built up some courage and then eased down into the water again. She dove under, groping about with her hands, trying to find the open hatch. There it was. She felt the opening. Rocks. Sand. Some sharp coral. She felt all around the opening, searched every inch of it, but found no good news at all. There simply was no open space she could escape through.

The pod had jammed itself into the ocean floor, burying the hatch.

Lila surfaced and cried out to God. She wailed out of anger, out of desperation, out of fear on the edge of panic.

Outside the pod, the deep blue waters of the Pacific surrounded the pod with stillness and silence. Not a sound could be heard.

Lila floated in the pod for a while, weeping, resting her head against the cold metal wall. How long would her oxygen bottle last? Did anyone even know where she was?

Once she had had such great hope, but felt only despair now. The knowledge of her situation was descending on her like a dark shroud of doom.

Her only way of escape was gone.

# SEVEN

Bad Dave kept his eyes on the stars and his hand on the big sailboat's tiller as the sloop knifed through the clear blue waters, heading for the small, obscure island of Tukani. Dr. Cooper, Jay, and Mrs. Flaherty slept away some of the hours and spent the rest of the time in conversation—there was much catching up to do.

"It's a nasty business these rebels are into," said Mrs. Flaherty, "and you can be sure the Soviets are behind them. I just regret that your daughter—and now you—have to be tossed into the middle of terrible trouble not your own."

Dr. Cooper had to smile. "That happens to us a lot, believe me. But what brings *you* into all this?"

She had to smile as well. "Oh, the trouble, of course! I *look* for it. I do investigative reporting for the major news syndicates, and the only way to report on something is to get involved in it."

"Well, now we're all involved together."

" 'And a threefold cord is not quickly broken.' "

Dr. Cooper recognized the quotation. "Ecclesiastes. You read the Bible?"

"It's God's Holy Word. I've grown up with it. Are you a person of faith yourself?"

Dr. Cooper nodded. "Without the Lord God to trust in, I don't think we could ever survive in times like this."

"Then we can all agree that Lila's in God's hands."

"And we can pray."

Mrs. Flaherty thought that was a wonderful idea. "That we can!"

And they did, the three of them, joining their hands together and asking God to protect Lila and to help them find her. Each had prayed many times before, but there was something very special about the three of them praying together; it brought a very special peace and a very special bond of faith and hope between them.

Then Dr. Cooper looked at his watch and gazed intently ahead, watching for the first glimpse of the island. "Now I'm even more hopeful. It's plain to see that the Lord is really guiding us, one step at a time."

"It's His way, isn't it? No matter where I go, I can be sure He's always with me."

Jay asked, "What does your husband do while you're traveling?"

Mrs. Flaherty smiled. "Oh, when I get to heaven I suppose I'll ask him. John passed away three years ago."

Jay was instantly embarrassed. "Oh . . . I'm sorry."

She quickly reassured him. "Think nothing of it. It was a fair question, and one I'm not shy to answer."

Jay felt relieved. "My mother died three years ago too."

Mrs. Flaherty was touched. "Well, we share the same sort of loss then." She looked at Dr. Cooper. "What was her name?"

But Dr. Cooper was looking ahead very intently, and for a moment Mrs. Flaherty wondered if he had heard the question. He finally answered, but it was as if the name had been pried out of him. "Katherine."

Jay told her, "We were all working at a dig in Egypt, and there was a cave-in. It was—"

"We don't talk about it much," Dr. Cooper interrupted.

Jay wanted to, but he could see the hard look in his father's eyes that he'd come to know all too well. He knew there could be no further discussion. "No," he softly agreed, "I guess we don't."

Mrs. Flaherty was studying Dr. Cooper's face, almost reading it. "I understand," she said finally.

Dr. Cooper didn't seem to hear her, but turned and called over his shoulder, "How are we doing, Dave?"

Dave answered, "Keep looking. We should be there by now if I've figured it right."

"Dad, I think I see it," said Jay.

"Off the port side, Dave," said Dr. Cooper.

"Right. That's Tukani."

The eastern sky was just turning red with the dawn as they approached Tukani. They could see that this island was bigger than Kurnoe, and even had some volcanic hills. Dave kept a very careful eye out for reefs, but the waters were clear of obstacles and approaching the island was easy. The waters soon became shallow.

"Here's as far as this boat goes," said Dave. "Jay, you can give me a hand."

Jay helped Dave lower the sails, and the sloop eased to a very gentle stop. Dave threw in the anchor.

Dr. Cooper was carefully surveying the beach. It would have made a beautiful vacation paradise, with smooth, white sand stretching as far as the eye could see in either direction, lazy, swaying palm trees, and the light of the moon reflected off the clear water like dancing, silver jewels. It would have been such a wonderful, enjoyable sight . . . except for the dull, thudding, frightening sound now reaching their ears, the distant beating of drums boom-boom-booming across the water, painting all kinds of fearsome pictures in their minds.

"The cannibals?" Jay ventured.

"One and the same," said Dave. "The drums of the Sutolos. But they sound far enough away, probably the other side of the island. If luck shines on us, they won't know we're here."

"But suppose this pearl diver is one of *them*," said Mrs. Flaherty. "We may have to walk right into their camp and present ourselves . . ."

"On a platter?" Jay ventured.

"Hold it," said Dave. "There might be more trouble."

He was looking out to sea, and now they could all hear the dull drone of a boat motor.

"There," said Dr. Cooper, pointing.

Dave grabbed his binoculars and took a better look. "Too dark to tell if they're friendly or not. I don't see them smiling, anyway."

"How big a boat is it?"

"Ehh . . . not too big, no bigger than ours, I think. But it has speed, and they're using all of it. They're in a hurry to get here."

Dr. Cooper looked around, trying to think of their options. "The Sutolos on one side, this unknown bunch on the other, and an unknown island in between . . ."

"I have some guns below," said Dave. "I say we bring them out."

Lila had time to rest on top of the wooden crate, out of the water, in the warm, red light cast from the control panel of the mysterious machine. She'd finally made an agreement with herself: No more desperation, hollering, or crying. Who would hear any of it anyway? No, there was only one proper way to spend her time and energy down here, and that was in figuring out some way to escape. After all, it just wasn't like a Cooper to give up.

So, having calmed herself, and having decided on how she would spend what might be the rest of her life, she began to explore the pod again.

She could still make it sway a little by shifting her weight back and forth. She took a wrench and tapped along the hull, listening for different sounds that might tell her anything. As near as she could tell, the top end was free in the water, while the bottom end was stuck in the ocean floor. So . . . if she could somehow open the top end, she should have a clear swim to the surface from there. If she expected to get out through the hatch, well, that would take some digging through the rock, coral, and sand.

She decided that digging would be her only chance. She had the crowbar. That might work.

Fitting the oxygen mask tightly over her face, she slipped into the water, ducked under the surface, and began to grope about for the tool bag. She found it, opened it, and took out the crowbar.

Then she began to explore the hatch opening. She tested the rocks and sand with the crowbar. There was definitely more rock and coral than sand, and nothing would give. She jammed the crowbar into the rock with great force, and one small chip broke away. At that rate it would take her ten years to get through. She jammed the crowbar into another spot and only hurt her hand.

She poked her head above the surface and rested for a moment. *No despair now, Lila. Keep calm.*

*How about anger?* she thought. *Lord, I have to feel something! You got me into this! What kind of a God are You anyway, to make people hurt and suffer like this?*

Then she thought, *Maybe it's my fault. Maybe I've sinned and God is punishing me.*

Something else came to her mind. Again she thought of her father, and the same old scenes flashed through her mind—scenes of her mother, alive, joyful, and loving, always there, a woman who really understood Lila's problems and questions, who really loved her children and her husband. And then came the later scenes of her father, alone, silent, unfeeling, unwilling to even mention her mother's name.

"I could just *hit* him!" she shouted to God. "I'm sorry, Lord, but that's just the way I feel! I *miss* Mom! I *miss* her, and I wish I could have her back!"

Well, there. She'd said it. She'd gotten that load off her mind and heart. All she could hope was that God wasn't mad at her for being disrespectful.

"And you know something else that hurts me, Lord?" she asked. "He never talks about her. I mean, you'd think she was never our mom, or that they'd never been married, or that they never even loved each other! You know what I can't help thinking? I get the feeling that he doesn't even *care!* I think he just wants to forget her, and that's . . . well, I think that's mean! It's cold, and it's hard! *Jay and I* loved her! *We* like to think about her and remember her! But You know what else I think!"

But she stopped short and didn't say it. She was disappointed in herself for even thinking such a thing.

But the thought was there, and the bitterness that came with it: *It's really his fault. It's his fault that she's dead. He's the one to blame.*

The strange boat was coming closer, its motor running full-speed, the white water bursting from its bow.

Dave, Dr. Cooper, and Mrs. Flaherty were armed now with rifles and sitting very low in Dave's boat, watching the other vessel approach.

"Ehhh . . ." said Dave, looking through his binoculars. "They might be American. They're white men, anyway."

"So are Russians!" said Mrs. Flaherty.

They found out soon enough. In just a few minutes, the speedy, thirty-foot craft came in close, the motor dropped to an idle, and the boat pulled in alongside them.

There were nine men in the boat, carrying sidearms and rifles. Some were dressed for rough action in the jungle, and some were dressed in wetsuits for underwater work. All of them looked very tough and threatening. As soon as they saw the rifles in the hands of the three in the big sailboat, they brandished their own weapons and made them look very obvious.

One man, apparently the group leader, stood up in the boat and called a greeting. "Good morning."

He sounded American.

Dave returned a "Good morning," then added, "And who might you be?"

"Lieutenant Joe Adams, and this is a special commando team from the *U.S.S. Findley*. I'd like to know who you people are."

Dave offered his hand and introduced everyone.

Lieutenant Adams got right to the point. "And just what is your business in these waters?"

"Same as it's always been," said Dave. "And up until today, nobody ever thought it was so important to come asking about it. What makes it so important to you?"

Adams got cold and demanding. "You haven't answered my question."

"Well, you haven't answered mine."

Dr. Cooper saw no purpose in this face-off. "Uh, gentlemen, if we could start over . . ."

"Jake," said Dave, "this man's nothing but an outsider, a no-good snooper, and I don't like him nudging his nose into our business!"

Dr. Cooper addressed the lieutenant. "Lieutenant, could we see some identification?"

Adams looked at his men with a queer expression. Apparently he'd never been asked that before. He had to get a pouch from below deck and dig around in it to find his black leather folder. He flipped it open and showed them all his identification. It was complete, even with a recent color photo; he was clearly who he said he was.

Dr. Cooper was satisfied. "Thank you. Now, are we suspected of a criminal trespass?"

"No," said Adams.

"Do you have authority to detain us?"

"If I find reasonable cause."

"Have you found it?"

"Not yet."

"Then let's talk a bit, on the same level. Either we can help each other out, or—"

"Or we can all shoot each other," said Dave.

"Dave . . ." Dr. Cooper cautioned, "rather than doing that, why don't you invite the lieutenant aboard your boat?"

Dave's mouth dropped open, and he was about to squawk. But Dr. Cooper just nodded assurance to him, and he softened.

"Okay," he said. "But just the lieutenant . . . and his feet better be clean!"

The lieutenant came aboard, and Dr. Cooper offered him a seat.

"Now," said Dr. Cooper. "I don't mind stating our business here. We're looking for my daughter. She was aboard an Air Force plane, en route to the United States, and it may have gone down in this area."

Dr. Cooper studied Adams's face for a reaction. There was a slight tightening in the jaw muscles, all right, but Adams kept a straight face otherwise.

Adams asked, "And how do you know where to look?"

"We don't know anything for sure. We're mainly following some flimsy leads and some strong hunches. But would you know anything about all this?"

Adams only nodded to his men, who immediately pointed all their guns at Dr. Cooper and the others. "I only need to tell you one thing. I've found reasonable cause to detain you for questioning, doctor. All of you are under arrest."

Three commandos jumped aboard the sailboat with their sidearms in hand to arrest them.

"Hand over your weapons," Adams ordered.

Dr. Cooper and the others obeyed, although Dave was the last. The three men snatched the guns away impatiently.

"All right, get aboard our boat. We'll have to take you back to the *Findley*—"

"Lieutenant!" one of the men yelled.

The lieutenant looked, as did the others, and they all saw another boat approaching at great speed.

"The Commies!" said Adams. "Get aboard the boat! Fast!"

Dr. Cooper, Jay, Dave, and Mrs. Flaherty, urged, pulled, and pushed by the commandos, clambered aboard the Navy craft as fast as they could.

"What about my boat?" Dave demanded.

"Too slow. We have to run for it!"

The Navy boat roared to life and shot forward with a lurch that knocked some of them to the deck. Kicking up a white wake, its bow slapping the water, it shot along, its new passengers hanging on for dear life.

Gunshots! Bullets began to punch holes in the walls of the boat. Adams and his men hit the deck and took defensive positions, their rifles ready.

An explosion! Dave looked back in time to see his precious sailboat blossom into a ball of fire and disintegrate into charred, fluttering fragments. All he could do was holler in anger and despair.

"They're using rockets," said Adams. "They mean business!"

They could all see the other boat getting closer. It was definitely Communist rebels, perhaps from Kurnoe, who were shooting at them, their guns flashing and smoking.

Another rocket sailed through the sky in a high arc, trailing a plume of smoke.

"Evade that thing!" Adams yelled, and the driver swerved the boat to and fro, trying to stay out of the rocket's way. The rocket finally dove into the ocean with a powerful explosion and a towering plume of white water.

"It's no good," said Adams. "They're gaining. They're going to catch us." He shouted an order to his men: "Open fire!"

The whole boat became a deafening chorus of gunfire, with rapid bursts and pops so loud you could feel them in your chest. Bullets were flying everywhere. Somewhere, somehow Dave managed to get his hands on a machine gun and began spraying bullets backward along with the others.

Another rocket exploded only fifteen feet away, the plume of water dousing them all.

The two boats roared along over the blue ocean, circling the island like two thundering hydroplanes, swerving, bouncing, slapping the water, exchanging volleys of gunfire and a steady pounding of exploding rockets.

A reef! Without warning, with incredible force, the Navy boat slammed into it and sailed into the air, the bow raised high, the stern dropping, dropping, the boat slowly flipping over. Thirteen bodies were flung out and tumbled like rag dolls into the ocean, hitting the water in a wide pattern of splashes. Then the Navy boat came down, plunging upside-down and stern-first into the ocean surface, where it broke apart in a cascade of white water and foam.

When Dr. Cooper's head broke the surface, he gasped for breath and looked around for his son.

"Dad!" came a call.

"Jay!" he answered.

They started swimming toward each other. They could see others swimming also.

"Doc," came Dave's voice. "You all right?"

"Over here," said Dr. Cooper.

The rebel boat slowed down in time to ease around the reef and then cruise in among all the swimming, struggling bodies. The hull of the boat had taken quite a beating from the Navy commandos' gunfire, but it was still afloat, and the rough-looking men on board were ready for more mischief. Dr. Cooper could recognize some of them—he'd seen them before on Kurnoe. Some he'd even fought with in that trade store scuffle.

But they were the winners now, grinning maliciously, their guns trained on the poor, splashing, struggling survivors of the wrecked Navy boat. They started taking prisoners. The chase was over.

# EIGHT

There was no sense in resisting. The rebels clearly had the upper hand, and even fired a few very close shots to make that fact abundantly clear. One by one, the Navy commandos were plucked from the water, wrestled into the boat, and disarmed, now captives under the muzzles of many rifles, their hands on their heads. A very large, bare-chested man reached down and snatched Jay out of the water like a freshly caught salmon, dropping him into the boat with no thought of courtesy. Mrs. Flaherty received no better treatment for being a woman. To make matters worse, some of the rebels were beginning to realize that she was the old cloth lady who had deceived them, and she could sense their desire to even the score. When Dr. Cooper was pulled on board, she drew close to him for protection and it seemed to work. The rebels left her alone, at least for the time being.

The rebels failed to pull Bad Dave aboard. He started swimming for the island as soon as his body hit the water, and by the time they had captured all the others, Dave was halfway to the shore.

No problem. The boat, laden with soldiers and captives, came in close to the shore and several rebels jumped into the shallow water to form a welcoming committee to greet Dave when he arrived.

When all the prisoners were finally in the boat,

secure and accounted for, the rebel commander clicked on the boat's radio and sent out a message.

Bad Dave told Dr. Cooper, "He just checked in with his boss and told him about us. I think the boss is coming here to see for himself."

That was all Dave could say before a guard grabbed him by his hair and hollered at him. Dr. Cooper couldn't understand all the language, but he had no trouble figuring out what the guard wanted: Dave was to keep his mouth shut.

They waited, not saying a word, sweating under the hot sun, cramped and uncomfortable in an over-crowded rebel boat now anchored just off the island of Tukani. An hour passed, and then another. Their clothes were sticky with salt, their hair was matted with seawater. They tried to behave themselves as best they could; it seemed that their captors grew more and more nervous with each passing minute.

Just then the first rebel spotted something in the distance and shouted to the others. They all looked and began to laugh and chatter excitedly.

The prisoners slowly twisted their heads around to have a look for themselves and saw a very large, very impressive yacht approaching, snow-white, sleek, at least eighty feet long, cutting through the water like a sharp knife.

Mrs. Flaherty figured the rebels were too busy chattering to hear her whisper to her friends, "So here comes the Soviet puppeteer, the man who pulls all the strings."

"And pads all the pockets," added Dave.

The big yacht grew and grew in size as it came nearer, its big engines rumbling, its twin stacks puffing black diesel smoke. The rebels piloted their boat out to meet the huge craft, and the two boats tied up along-side each other, the big yacht so large it made the rebels' little craft look like a toy. The crewmen aboard the yacht were mostly Polynesian and Filipino, but there was no question about the nationality of the skipper, the imposing, straight-standing man who appeared on the bridge.

"Russian," said Dave.

"Big Daddy himself," said Dr. Cooper.

The Russian looked down at the miserable contents of the rebel boat and smiled a cruel smile. He shouted a question in Filipino to the rebel commander.

"He wants to know who our leaders are," said Dave.

The rebel commander pointed at Lieutenant Adams and then at Dr. Cooper.

The Russian gave an order, and immediately the rebel guards yanked Dr. Cooper and Adams to their feet, along with Mrs. Flaherty, Dave, and Jay. A crewman on the yacht lowered a ladder, and they were forced to climb aboard one by one. When they stepped over the railing, they were greeted by more armed guards who escorted them aft. There, under a large awning, they were allowed to sit in comfortable deck chairs.

The Russian skipper looked them over carefully with cold, blue eyes, and then he spoke.

"I am Mr. Ivanovich, of the Union of Soviet Socialist Republics—the KGB, to be exact. Who am I addressing?"

"Lieutenant Joe Adams, U.S. Navy, serial number—"

"Fine, lieutenant, fine," said Ivanovich. "I know the rest." He looked at Dr. Cooper. "And you?"

Dr. Cooper introduced himself and the others as well.

"And what are you doing in the company of this military man?"

Dr. Cooper answered simply, "He arrested us."

"Oh, but you *are* the Americans who were recently on the island of Kurnoe, correct?"

Dr. Cooper remained silent.

Ivanovich was undaunted. "I understand there was quite a brawl in the trade store over a . . . snail eating contest?" He laughed at that and then looked at Mrs. Flaherty. "And this would be the old cloth lady, hm?" He smiled at Jay. "And this would be the young fighter I've heard so much about." He stood tall, looked at them all, and declared, "Quite a catch. So far I'm having a wonderful day."

He then took a chair himself, facing his captives, openly gloating over his luck.

"Well, Lieutenant Adams," he said, "I suppose you've told your friends what this whole, exciting game is all about?"

"I'm Lieutenant Joe Adams, U.S. Navy, serial number—"

"Never mind. I'll tell them myself. Dr. Cooper, am I correct in thinking you're looking for a particular American aircraft? A U.S. Air Force C-141?"

Dr. Cooper didn't answer.

Ivanovich just kept going. "Well, so are we; that should be obvious. But let me tell you why, and then Lieutenant Adams can verify whether or not I'm telling you the truth.

"Doctor, you might recall, some time ago, a violent explosion, a brilliant fireball, appearing in the skies over Japan, China, the entire Orient. It was in all the papers. Do you recall that event at all?"

Dr. Cooper acknowledged, "I did read about it."

"Good, good. Then let me explain what really happened. You see, that was not a meteor burning in the atmosphere as the media claimed. No, that explosion was man-made. It was a secret test of an immensely powerful, ground-based, anti-satellite laser, a weapon designed to destroy enemy satellites and ballistic missiles. The test was, as you can guess, a remarkable success. The laser was able to completely destroy a large, orbiting target some four hundred miles in space. A weapon of such precision and power would clearly put the United States decades ahead of the Soviet Union in strategic defense weaponry.

"At any rate, a secret test that causes brilliant explosions in space can't remain a secret for very long, and it didn't. My government found out about the weapon, they want it, and they have commissioned me to get it for them, as quietly as possible, and without involving Soviet forces directly. That wouldn't look good to the rest of the world, you understand.

"So my plan was to hire someone else to get it. These fine defenders of the oppressed, these fighters for the liberation of the Philippines, were only too willing to make a contract with us to secure the weapon, and we are, of course, paying them handsomely in money and weapons to use in their own cause. That way, they get what they want and we get what we want while the world goes on thinking that the Soviet Union is only interested in peace and not conquest."

Ivanovich turned to Adams and asked, "Am I telling the truth so far?"

Adams wouldn't say a word.

Ivanovich was impressed. "You are a very loyal American, Lieutenant Adams. Fortunately for us, the two men aboard that plane, Max Baker and Al Reed, were not, and we were able to buy their loyalty. As you may have guessed, the laser was aboard that plane, en route to the United States for further testing and refinement. Hijacking the plane was an easy and logical plan, and it did work well . . . up to a point."

Ivanovich leaned back and sighed. "And that's why we're all here, isn't it? That plane, with its precious cargo, was supposed to land at the rebuilt airstrip on Kurnoe, the laser was supposed to be transferred to a Soviet plane and carried away, the C-141 was supposed to be destroyed at sea . . . Ah, it would have been so smooth, so perfect."

Ivanovich paused to think about the scheme that didn't work and then concluded, "Instead, the plane has vanished, and we all find ourselves in a race to find that laser—a massive treasure hunt, winner take all."

The Russian leaned forward and gave Dr. Cooper a piercing gaze. "But that brings us to you, Dr. Cooper, and your comrades here, the boy and the cloth lady. You do have some information, don't you?"

Dr. Cooper only smiled and shook his head. "Mr. Ivanovich, I wish I did."

Ivanovich did not soften. "You do, Dr. Cooper. I am sure of it. That native in the trade store on Kurnoe, the poor man who couldn't keep down all those snails . . . He gave you a locket, did he not?"

"I can tell you weren't there."

"And he told you where he found it, didn't he? He told you where to look for the lost aircraft."

"That would have been nice."

"And that is why you slipped away so hurriedly in the night, to come here to this island to find that plane. Now tell me, where is the plane? Where were you planning to look?"

"Why didn't you ask that native?"

Ivanovich leaned back. "We did. Unfortunately, he died a very cruel death at the hands of our interrogators before he would consent to tell us." Then he jerked forward and shouted the words right into Dr. Cooper's face. "And you will die too, doctor, if you do not tell us everything we wish to know!"

Lila was up to her neck in silty, muddy seawater, exhausted, and finally beginning to accept that she would *never* be able to dig herself out. She'd been hacking and chopping away for hours at the ocean floor that blocked the hatch, but she'd really accomplished little more than using up her oxygen and dirtying up the water that filled the bottom of the pod.

With slow, painful exertion, she climbed out of the filth and eased slowly up to her perch atop the big wooden crate. She flopped down and lay there, limp, getting used to the idea of failing at this attempt.

"Boy, Lord," she said out loud, "I wonder if anyone even knows I'm down here. Sure, I know *You* do, but . . . who else? I mean, here I am, all alone with my problem, and I don't even know if anyone out there knows about it or even cares! As a matter of fact, I'm not even sure that *You* care!"

God didn't seem to be answering her at the moment. Maybe His phone was off the hook. Maybe He was tired of listening to her cries.

"Lord . . . all I want to do is get out of this trap. Can't You see that?"

But that question brought a memory back to Lila's mind. She fell silent and let the memory replay before her eyes.

"He's trapped, Lila, trapped inside his own feelings." Her mother had said that, years ago. Lila could remember the place: a quiet, breezy park in England, with green lawns, a large pond with swans, huge weeping willows. Lila was only nine or ten, and she'd been crying. She and her mother were sitting on a park bench, and her mother was holding her close and comforting her. Her mother was beautiful; the sun was making her long, blonde hair shimmer like gold.

"Sometimes," her mother said, "people get hard on the outside because they're very hurt on the inside. They don't want to be hurt anymore, so they hide inside a shell."

Lila could remember it all so vividly. She lay there in the dim red light, her eyes vacant, just watching the memory like a movie.

Then her mother had said something like, "He didn't mean to be angry toward you, not at all. You just need to understand your father. Whenever he gets really hurt, well, he buries himself in whatever he's doing and it takes him a while to dig himself out again. Do you understand?"

Lila tried to remember if she'd understood at the time. She didn't think so. As nearly as she could remember, she was angry and hurt toward her father about something. Just what was it, anyway?

Oh brother. Now she remembered. She wanted him to take her to the park, but he said he couldn't, and he seemed like he was upset about something, and Lila thought he was mad at her, and . . .

Lila winced. Oh, that's right. That was when the university cut back his funding because he was taking the Bible too seriously. Boy, no wonder he was upset.

Then Lila became still and listened to her own thoughts taking form: *He was hurt very badly, but I didn't see it. I only thought he was being unkind to me. I thought he didn't care about me.*

Then she knew. "Lord, it's You, isn't it? *You're* reminding me of these things! Help me, Lord. Help me to hear what You're saying."

Some of her own words came back to her mind: *"Lord, all I want to do is get out of this trap . . . Here I am, all alone with my problem, and I don't even know if anyone out there knows about it, or even cares . . ."*

She thought about those words, and it occurred to her that they not only applied to her . . . They might apply to her father as well. Was he hurting too? Did anyone else know or even care? Did *she* care?

"Lord," she asked, "is that why he never talks about Mom?"

Dr. Cooper remained firm and steady under the gaze of the Soviet agent trying to scare him.

"Mr. Ivanovich," he said, "you're a powerful Soviet with all the manpower, machinery, transportation, and weapons you could ask for. What could you possibly need from us?"

Lieutenant Adams jumped in. "Cooper, don't talk to this man! He's the enemy!"

"Silence!" Ivanovich shouted. "Dr. Cooper is wise to be talking. He will spare his life, and maybe *your* lives, by cooperating."

Adams persisted, "That laser is the property of the United States. We can't let the Soviets steal it!"

"I didn't come here because of the laser," said Dr. Cooper. "I came to find my daughter."

Ivanovich raised his eyebrows at that. "Your daughter?"

"She was aboard that plane as well. My friends and I came here only to look for her. We knew nothing about any laser weapon."

Ivanovich smiled wickedly. "Dr. Cooper, we know good and well that there were no civilian passengers scheduled on that flight."

"No, not at first. Lila was scheduled in at the last minute. It would have been too late for your people to find out about it."

Then Ivanovich laughed loudly. "Yes, Dr. Cooper, of course! Here we are, the two greatest world powers, searching for the most powerful deterrent to nuclear attack ever devised in this atomic age, a weapon that could put one nation well ahead of the other in defense technology, and you insist you are only concerned with finding a lost child? You actually expect me to believe that?"

Jay blurted, "But it's true!"

Ivanovich chuckled. "Oh, come now! We are talking about sheer, raw *power,* superior tactical weaponry. No single human life can be more important than that!"

Now Jay was ready to preach, and even stood to his feet. "My sister *is* important! God loves her and we love her, and she's lost and in trouble, and that means we have to find her and save her. But all you guys can think about is that stupid laser, just another way to blow each other up!"

Ivanovich smiled and replied, "Young man, that is because the power of the many, the Soviet Union, is far more important than the life of just one, your sister."

"Well, that's wrong!"

Ivanovich looked at Dr. Cooper with fire in his eyes. "You allow your son to be so disrespectful?"

Dr. Cooper's answer was firm. "I've raised my son to respect his elders . . . But I've also raised him to speak the truth."

Ivanovich nodded, but his eyes were filled with an evil craftiness. He looked at Jay again, studying him for a moment.

"So he likes to speak the truth, does he? And you think that a life is beyond price? Very well. We'll see how strongly you all believe that."

Jay could not overpower or escape from the two strong men who were tying him down, lashing him to the rocks with thick ropes. The waves of the incoming tide were washing and swirling around the rocks, reaching as high as Jay's waist. The men cinched the ropes tight and made their way back toward the shore.

On the beach, Ivanovich and five of his rebel henchmen made sure that Dr. Cooper, Mrs. Flaherty, Dave, and Lieutenant Adams watched every detail.

"It will only be a matter of hours," said Ivanovich. "The waves will help him think about what his own life might be worth. They will keep rising, inch by inch, until the tide covers him, and then . . . well, he will drown. Perhaps before that happens, he or one of you—will be persuaded to tell me what I want to know."

"Don't say a word," said Adams.

But Dr. Cooper could only think about Jay and watch in agony as wave after wave, each one just a little higher, washed over his helpless son.

# NINE

*Clunk!* A rock bounded off a rebel's head, and he crumbled to the sand.

*Zip! Zip!* Two more guards cried out in pain, stuck in their necks by small feathered darts.

Lieutenant Adams, hit by a stone, collapsed to the beach, dazed, and then flopped facedown in the sand, unconscious.

Dr. Cooper and the others instinctively dropped to the sand. The four remaining rebel guards did not, but pointed their rifles toward the jungle.

*Zip!* went two more darts. *Clunk!* went another rock. Three more fell to the sand. The last one fired about five shots before a rock *and* a dart dropped him.

And then it was over, so fast and so quietly that Dr. Cooper and the others hardly had time to realize what had happened before the grasses and bushes parted and a large band of hideous savages stepped out onto the beach. They were almost naked, wearing only woven grass skirts around their waists and seashells around their necks. They were grim-looking, carrying blowguns to fire darts, slings for hurling stones, and long, deadly-looking spears. There were at least thirty of them, easily outnumbering the small, helpless party of white strangers on the beach.

Without his armed men Ivanovich was helpless and obviously alarmed, and Dave noticed. "Hey, Ivanovich, how much is *your* life worth? These are the Sutolos. They *eat* Russians!"

Ivanovich wasn't too happy about that idea. He tried to run back to the launch that had brought them all here, but two husky warriors were more fleet of foot and grabbed him before he could escape. They carried him back, holding him off the ground in their thick arms. He struggled, but only managed to kick the air.

Other warriors grabbed Dr. Cooper, Mrs. Flaherty, and Dave and lifted them forcibly to their feet, holding them in an iron grip.

"Dave," said Dr. Cooper, "can you speak Sutolo?"

"Uh . . . *'Mem bay goonai techam.'* How's that?"

"What does it mean?"

" 'Please pass the salt,' I think."

Dave's Sutolo didn't impress any of the powerful warriors that now surrounded them. As the captives watched, two of the warriors, apparently leaders, turned the fallen rebels over, inspected them, and then shook their heads, muttering.

"What are they doing?" Ivanovich asked, his voice trembling.

"Deciding who to have for dinner," said Dave. "And I hope they pick *you!*"

"You are joking!"

"We'll see, Ruskie, we'll see!"

The two Sutolos didn't seem to like Lieutenant Adams either and passed him by.

But then they came to Mrs. Flaherty, took one look at her, and smiled broadly, exchanging rolling, tumbling syllables as they pinched her arms and discussed the meat on her bones. They began to nod to each other, very pleased.

"I was afraid of that," said Dave.

"I'm not flattered," said Mrs. Flaherty.

The two gave some orders, and the men holding Mrs. Flaherty took her aside.

Dave was next. They took a quick look at him and expressed some doubt, but they eventually nodded to the men holding him, and he too was taken aside to join Mrs. Flaherty.

Dr. Cooper looked at Ivanovich and said, "Well, now it's either you or me, or both of us."

The two "inspectors" stepped up to have a look at Ivanovich. One pinched his cheek, and Ivanovich was humiliated. They began to mutter to each other. They sounded positive.

"Wait," said Ivanovich. "Wait, I can make a deal with you!"

The two warriors looked at each other and stared blankly at Ivanovich.

Ivanovich struggled against the guards holding him, trying to pull back the cuff of his sleeve. "Look! Look at this!" He was finally able to hold his arm out and point to his gold wristwatch. "Take this! Take this, not me!"

The two warriors looked at the watch, but didn't seem too impressed.

Just then, Ivanovich got another idea. He pointed frantically toward the waves. "Look! I have a boy! A young, tender boy! See there?"

The two savages looked out toward the rocks and saw Jay, still tied down, struggling for breaths of air between waves.

"Take the watch and take *him!* Deal?"

The warriors mumbled to each other about it, looked at Ivanovich, and then at Jay. They thought for a moment.

Then they nodded, gave an order, and the two men holding Ivanovich let him go and went out into the surf to get Jay. The two savage leaders took Ivanovich's watch and then shoved him aside as something unfit to eat. He was quite pleased with their decision.

They chose Dr. Cooper with hardly a glance, and Ivanovich was pleased with that decision too.

Ivanovich hurried to the launch. "Well and good, American friends. You did manage to avoid revealing your secrets to me, but now it seems you won't be in the race to find the laser either, and I'm satisfied with that. I hope you won't mind if I leave rather hurriedly. I think it's dinnertime for these people, and I hate to intrude. Farewell."

Ivanovich climbed into the launch and pushed out from the shore, starting up the motor and leaving behind his fallen men.

The Sutolos were satisfied with their catch and headed back into the jungle, dragging along Dr. Cooper, Jay, Mrs. Flaherty, and Bad Dave. When they came to a trail, the warriors let go of their prisoners, and they all continued hiking through the jungle, heading for the other side of the island. The Sutolo drums could be heard in the distance, pounding out a steady, throbbing beat like distant thunder.

Jay was soaking wet and a little cold, but he just kept walking, hoping the exercise would keep him warm. His father was walking between the two leaders of the war party just ahead, and Jay kept watching him in case he might try to give some kind of signal, some tip on how they might escape. So far, there seemed to be no way out of this.

Oh! What was this? Jay was startled to find a blanket dropped on his shoulders. A big warrior just behind him, a fearsome man with a bone through his nose, helped him wrap it around himself.

The two big men escorting Dr. Cooper were mumbling to each other about something when the big bald one on the right extended his arm to display Ivanovich's gold wristwatch. His friend, a shaggy young man with a missing tooth, was impressed and chuckled with pleasure. The bald man seemed concerned about something, however, and took the watch from his wrist so he could tinker with it. Then both men started passing it back and forth, muttering and mumbling strange words to each other. Apparently they were in disagreement as to what the strange object was for. They held it this way, then that, turned it over, shook it, and put it to their ears to listen to it, but they could not come to an agreement.

Finally the shaggy one poked Dr. Cooper with his big fat finger and asked, "Do you know how to set this thing?"

Dr. Cooper heard it, but couldn't believe he'd heard it. He only stared at the big Sutolo with wide eyes.

"You *do* speak English?" the Sutolo asked him.

"Why . . . yes," said Dr. Cooper, finally finding his tongue.

The Sutolo handed him the watch. "We're in a different time zone here, one hour later."

Dr. Cooper took the watch, and all he could say was, "Oh." He inspected the watch and decided he'd just explain it. "This is a digital watch, battery-powered. Here. You press these little buttons on the side to set it . . ."

He just kept going, telling them all about the watch. He was more than happy to help them out. They were communicating—that was the important thing.

Jay had overheard the conversation and stole a glance back at the big warrior who had put the blanket over him.

"Warm enough?" the big man asked.

"Yes. Thank you very much."

The trail descended down the other side of the island and finally emerged from the jungle and into a very large village of grass huts and shelters erected on poles. The drums were loud and clear now, and the prisoners could see the drummers all sitting in a circle around a large bonfire in the center of the village, pounding away and singing happily. At least two hundred Sutolos, from warriors to mothers to children to fishermen, were gathered there, singing, chanting, laughing, and having quite a joyous meeting. When a young boy on the outside of the vast group saw the returning war party, he announced it loudly, pointing and jumping up and down, and the whole tribe of Sutolos looked toward them, chattering and laughing excitedly as the drumming stopped.

Dr. Cooper and the others were holding their breath now, not knowing what to expect. Were these people happy to see them out of hospitality . . . or hunger?

The crowd converged on them as the warriors held their spears aloft triumphantly, shaking them and hollering victorious words.

Several Sutolos reached for Mrs. Flaherty with their big brown hands. She shrank back, but then noticed that the hands stopped short of her body and remained open. She extended her hand very cautiously. They shook hers in greeting.

Then the captives heard a familiar voice from just beyond the crowd: "All right, all right, let a man through, come on now!"

The crowd parted, and a jolly, chubby fellow stepped forward, dressed in a grass skirt and a wide-brimmed straw hat.

Bad Dave hollered the name first. "Jerry! Reverend Jerry Garrison! What are you doing here?"

Jerry Garrison, the missionary from the island of Kurnoe, stepped up to the captives, a big smile on his face. "Oh, I came here in my own boat. I left Kurnoe about an hour after you did, as soon as I put some dummies in all our beds for the rebels to spend their time sneaking up on."

Dr. Cooper shook Jerry's hand, but had to make sure of one thing. "I take it we're going to live?"

Jerry laughed. "Oh yeah, sure, all . . . all *four* of you?" He looked the four of them over and then asked the two Sutolo leaders, "Suktay, Zebu! I thought I told you to bring *five* people back. Where's that other guy?"

Suktay and Zebu looked at each other and then tried to explain. "These are the only good people we saw. All the others were gun men, people who kill."

"No," said Jerry, "that other guy, he wasn't a bad man. He just looked like a bad man. Had a uniform, right? The color of leaves?"

They nodded and then very sheepishly explained, "We thought he was a bad man. We conked him in the head."

"You what?" Jerry cried. "You weren't supposed to knock *him* out! That was a friend, some Navy guy. Go get him too. And hurry, before those Commies wake up."

Suktay and Zebu gathered a party of six men, and they all bounded back toward the jungle.

"Oh, and Zebu!" Jerry called. The warrior turned. "Nice watch you have there!"

"Russian!" Zebu called. "Runs on batteries!"

They all disappeared into the jungle.

"All right, everybody," Jerry hollered. "Worship service is over. Just go ahead with your supper." Then he gave the same order in Sutolo.

The crowd broke up, and each family returned to its shelter. The warriors shook hands with their former captives and also went to their homes.

"Follow me," said Jerry, and he led the way through the village. "Don't worry about your Navy friend. I told the boys to be careful with their slings. The worst thing any of those men will have is a headache—except for the ones who got darted. That was sleep potion on those darts. They'll wake up in an hour or two, but then they'll be too silly to give us any trouble for the rest of the day."

"So don't tell me," said Dr. Cooper. "Let me guess. You've already done mission work among these people?"

"Oh sure, I've known them for years."

Bad Dave was getting hot under the collar. "So what about all this cannibal stuff you were handing us?"

"Oh, I wasn't kidding. I haven't been able to convert all these people, you know, and I couldn't be sure what they would do to strangers. I didn't know when I'd be able to get here to tell them you were my friends, so I figured I'd better keep you on your guard."

"You're a rascal, Rev. Garrison!" said Mrs. Flaherty.

"I saved your necks, didn't I? We were all watching the Commies getting the better of you out there. I figured they had no quarrel with the local natives, so I told the warriors to make it look convincing."

"We were convinced, all right," said Jay.

"And so was Ivanovich," said Dr. Cooper. "He was thankful just to leave us and get away."

"But what about those other Navy men?"

"Ivanovich and the rebels still have them."

"Well . . . we'll just pray that the Lord works something out to spring them. So far I can't think of a thing."

Jerry led them to a little grass hut on stilts, in the center of the village. "This is my place. It may not look like much, but it's my castle, my parsonage."

They all climbed the steep steps and went inside. Jerry had it furnished with just a few comforts: a cot, a small cookstove, a little desk made from packing crates. There was a picture of Jesus on the wall.

"Sit down and rest," he said, and they all did.

Then Jerry pulled something out from under the cot and set it in front of Dr. Cooper and Jay. They recognized it immediately.

It was Lila's suitcase, nicked, dented, scraped, and water-damaged.

Dr. Cooper opened it. Most of the contents were gone.

Jerry explained, "Suktay and Zebu brought it to

me the moment I mentioned your daughter. I'm afraid most of Lila's clothes and belongings have been taken and traded away by the local scavengers, but this is quite a find. It shows we're getting very close!"

"Where did it come from?"

"Who else? Kolo, the old pearl diver. I have some men out looking for him now."

Lila brushed the walls of the pod with her hand, gathering the condensation into drips large enough to direct into her mouth. First she gathered the moisture from one side of the pod and then the other, desperate for every drop she could gather and drink.

And with each precious drop, a gift from God in itself, she felt a gratitude building in her heart until tears filled her eyes and she began to weep.

She was becoming very well acquainted with gnawing hunger and raging thirst.

*I never thought a drop of water would mean so much to me,* she thought. *Lord, we just take so many things for granted and never thank You for what You provide. Thank You, Lord, for this drink off these walls. Thank You for keeping me alive this long and not forsaking me. Thank You for putting up with me when I pout and kick against You and want things my own way. I'm sorry, Lord, for hurting You.*

But now she could remember so vividly how she must have hurt someone else—her father. She could see herself again, spouting words of anger and hatred at him, accusing him of terrible things: "You never loved Mom at all! The only person you ever think about is yourself, you and all your little projects!"

She winced as she remembered more and more of her words: "Well, I've had it! I'm tired of you dragging me all over the world to help you do all your digging! I'm not your slave, I'm your daughter—and I deserve better, and I think *Mom* deserved better, if that makes any difference to you! I want to go home! I'm not going to stay in Japan one more day just so you can ignore me and take me for granted like you took Mom for granted!"

He didn't argue with her or scold her or even raise his voice. He only said, "I'll call Colonel Griffith. Maybe he can get you on a plane tomorrow."

Lila had remembered enough. She lay down on top of the wooden crate, turned her face toward the wall, and wept. Her family had been split apart, and the last thing any of them remembered was all the bad feelings and harmful words. Was this the way it would end?

"Lord," she finally said out loud, "thank You for Dad and Jay, and thank You that they really do love me no matter how rotten I've been toward them. I'm sorry for hurting them. I'm sorry that I've only been thinking about myself and how I feel and haven't thought about how others might be hurting." She had to pause to breathe and steady herself before she could go on. "Jesus . . . if You'll just get me out of here . . . I want to tell Dad I'm sorry. I'm sorry, Lord Jesus. Please let me tell him!"

# TEN

Dr. Cooper, Jay, Bad Dave, and Mrs. Flaherty were Jerry Garrison's honored guests in his little hut, and the Sutolos were showing them every kindness and comfort. They all had a chance to bathe, and the Sutolos brought them all fresh clothing—a slightly large, secondhand pair of trousers for Dr. Cooper, a pair of store-bought beach pants for Jay, a woven grass skirt for Bad Dave, and a beautiful, flowery sarong for Mrs. Flaherty—and had taken their clothes to one of the many clear streams for washing. The evening meal, brought by several Sutolo wives, was a very satisfying seafood and fruit banquet they were more than ready for.

"Remember to save some for what's-his-name," said Jerry.

"Lieutenant Joe Adams," said Dr. Cooper.

"Just how does he fit into this?"

"Government killjoy," said Dave. "That goon tried to arrest us!"

Dr. Cooper tried to give a truthful answer. "I think he and his men are an advance party from a Navy ship, the *U.S.S. Findley*. They're here looking for the Starlifter, just like the rest of us."

"Well, they didn't get too far, did they?" said Jerry.

"No. His men are still prisoners of the rebels, and I just don't know what can be done about that."

Bad Dave bit into a papaya and mumbled through

the mess in his mouth, "Well, I'll start helping Adams when he starts helping *us*."

Jerry saw something through the door of the hut. "Speaking of Adams . . ."

They all looked and saw a bizarre sight. With drums pounding out an announcement and Sutolos running to watch, Suktay and Zebu came into the village, chins high and chests out, leading their parade of proud warriors as if they were returning from a glorious victory.

There, looking like slain game, hanging by his wrists and ankles from a long pole carried on the shoulders of two warriors, was Lieutenant Joe Adams, dazed and indignant, the prize catch of the day!

Dr. Cooper and the others were so struck by the sight, they didn't know whether to be disgusted or to laugh.

"Mmm, some old customs are hard to change," Jerry admitted with a shrug of his shoulders. "Come on, let's help the poor guy out."

They hurried down and out of Jerry's hut in time to intercept the returning war party. Suktay and Zebu strode up to Jerry, all grins, and bowed deeply, presenting Adams as a special gift.

Jerry was quick to praise them. "Well done, Suktay and Zebu, and all the rest of you! That's a fine trophy you've brought!"

Adams was tired of being a trophy. "Hey! Talk some sense into these savages, will you?"

Bad Dave had some talking of his own to do. "Well now, let's not be so hasty! Maybe we need to talk some sense into *you* first!"

Adams glared at Dave. "I won't be taken advantage of, mister, and I certainly won't talk to anyone while hanging upside-down!"

Dave just shouted to the warriors, "Okay, throw him in the pot! Dinner's late as it is!"

The warriors meant well. They started to obey.

"No, no, wait!" Adams shouted.

Dr. Cooper stepped in. "Hold it, friends." The warriors set Adams down again. Dr. Cooper knelt to talk to him. "I'm glad to see you alive, sir."

Adams didn't know how to take that. "Well . . . so am I."

"I think Dave is trying to impress upon you that we all need to cooperate with each other, and I quite agree. You could say that all of us are—if you'll pardon the expression—stewing in the same pot. We're all after the same thing, we're all having the same trouble getting it, and we all have the same enemies."

Adams let that sink in. "So what are you proposing?"

"Well, I'm sure you have information useful to us, and we now have some native contacts that would be useful to you. As far as brute strength is concerned, both of us are without manpower and weapons. Our only resources are each other. If you'll forget about your official duty to arrest us, and work with us instead, maybe we can all see our goals realized together."

Adams thought about it. He also considered how much power he now had to arrest anyone, hanging from a pole. He asked all of them, "Are we all on the same side, with the best interests of the United States at heart?"

They all nodded. Bad Dave started singing, "My country, 'tis of thee, sweet land of liberty . . ."

"All right, all right," said Adams. "Agreed. We'll work together."

Jerry spoke to the warriors carrying Adams, and they carefully cut him loose.

"Come inside, lieutenant," said Jerry. "We have dinner waiting for you."

But just then there was a shout from the other end of the village, and they all looked to see yet another parade coming toward them.

Jerry shouted with glee, "Kolo! They've found him!"

Kolo, a little bald man with a wide, white smile and wiry limbs, was hurrying toward them, followed by several Sutolos carrying all kinds of objects that the Americans immediately recognized.

Adams could hardly contain his excitement. "He's found the plane!"

Jerry cautioned them all, "Don't rush toward him, please. Let him come to us. Be patient."

They followed Jerry's advice, but as the little man walked up to Jerry and shook hands, chattering away in Sutolo, their eyes were riveted on the many items the Sutolos were setting out in neat rows on the ground: small containers and boxes clearly labeled "USAF," some flight bags with the crewmen's names clearly visible, several tools, a spent oxygen bottle, an uninflated life raft.

Adams stepped forward and began to open one of the flight bags. The little pearl diver screamed indignantly and grabbed him. Adams threw him off.

Jerry shouted, "No, lieutenant, please! Get back!"

Lieutenant Adams suddenly felt a sharp prick in his back and froze. It was a spear point. Now there were several spears pointed at him from all sides. The Sutolos were ready to finish him right then and there.

Jerry chattered rapidly and desperately in the Sutolo tongue, trying to explain, trying to calm everyone. He gently took Adams by the arm and said, "Please step away. This is very insulting to them."

"This is U.S. Air Force property!" he protested.

"No—not the way they see it," said Jerry. "Please stand with the others."

Adams obeyed. The many warriors with their deadly spears made that decision easy.

Jerry continued to speak to the Sutolos and to the little pearl diver, trying to explain the misunderstanding, trying to apologize. They discussed the matter with him and seemed to accept what he was saying. Finally Jerry turned back to the Americans while the Sutolos and Kolo the pearl diver continued to arrange all the objects on the ground.

Jerry said quietly, "They have accepted your apology."

"Apology!" said Adams.

Jerry wouldn't let him say another word. "I have told them you are sorry for not respecting their ways, and they now understand that you are from a strange land far away and don't know any manners."

"Yeah," said Dave, glaring at Adams. "I'd say that's about right."

Jerry jumped in to explain before these two got into a scuffle. "Listen, everyone—Kolo considers himself a merchant and thinks you people have come here to buy his treasures from him. That's why he's putting them on display here for you to see."

"But it's not his property!" Adams protested quietly.

"Oh, but it *is*. According to Sutolo customs, if you pull something from the sea, it is yours, and not claimed by any man."

"From the *sea?*" asked Dr. Cooper.

Jerry saw that Kolo was ready. "I'll let him tell you about it." He spoke to Kolo in Sutolo, and Kolo began his sales pitch to these foreigners. The little man was very colorful in his little speech, with wide, flowing gestures and dramatic tones. He would have made a terrific salesman in the States.

Jerry translated Kolo's words. "These are rare treasures from Kolo's secret place beneath the sea. These are pieces of stars, of planets, of the great birds that roar through the heavens. None have seen such wonders before, nor shall they ever again. And today, American savages, I will make you a wonderful deal . . ."

The sales pitch went on and on. They were all very,

very impatient for Kolo to finish his speech so they could look at what he had brought, but until he finished there was nothing they could do but try to look attentive.

Finally Kolo ended his pitch with a bow, and Jerry finished the speech in English. "So come now, and look upon the treasures of Kolo, the magic riches that fell from the sky." Jerry added his instruction, "You may examine Kolo's wares, but please be very polite, and don't handle things too much."

They slowly and courteously approached the articles now lying in neat rows on the ground.

"So they fell from the sky," said Dr. Cooper.

"And came from beneath the sea," said Adams. "Doctor, I'm sorry, but it doesn't look good. Captain Weisfield may have tried to ditch the plane, but all these loose items indicate the plane disintegrated on impact. You'll notice the uninflated life raft. It's normally stowed near the rear escape hatch and deployed after a ditch. Apparently there were no survivors to deploy it."

Jay found something and brought it to his father. "Dad . . . here's Lila's handbag."

Dr. Cooper recognized it immediately and almost regretted seeing it. With Kolo's permission, they opened it. It was empty now. Kolo had probably already sold the contents, just as he had sold Lila's locket to the native on Kurnoe. But the initials, "L.M.C.," were plain enough.

"Jerry," Dr. Cooper asked, "can Kolo tell us anything about the crash site, anything about the condition of the plane?"

Jerry engaged Kolo in conversation. Kolo seemed willing to answer some questions, but shook his head in answer to others, unwilling to talk.

Jerry reported, "He says the treasures are not all in one place, but are spread out over a wide area on the ocean floor. He won't tell me exactly where. That's his secret cache and he doesn't want it pirated."

Adams shook his head. "Sounds like the plane broke apart." He asked Jerry, "Has he seen any sign of the plane itself, any parts of it?"

Jerry had to ask, "Uh . . . what does it look like?"

"Large, swept-wing, four-engine aircraft . . . high-wing configuration, about 160 feet long . . ."

"What color?"

"Uh . . . drab green."

Jerry talked some more to Kolo, and Kolo chattered back.

Jerry reported, "Kolo is suspicious. He suggests that you've been spying on his secret cache."

"We've hit a nerve," said Dr. Cooper. "He's seen what we're talking about."

"Tell him we haven't been spying. Tell him the plane is ours," said Adams.

"I will," said Jerry in a quiet tone. "But please, no more questions just yet. If we feed his suspicions, he'll stop cooperating altogether."

"But . . ." was all Jay could say. He exchanged a look with his father, and they were both feeling the same anguish: they were *so close!* They just couldn't be turned away now!

"Let's have a thorough look at all this debris," said Adams. "We might learn something, and it'll give this huckster time to decide he can trust us."

Adams turned to look in a native basket that was filled with smaller odds and ends. He came across a small object that caused his brow to wrinkle with curiosity.

Dr. Cooper joined him, as did Jay and Mrs. Flaherty. Adams had found a small metal tool shaped like a *T.*

"What is it?" Jay asked.

Adams explained, "It's the sealing key from the

weapons pod." He could see their quizzical looks, so he explained, "The . . ." He hesitated. "Oh, all right. Ivanovich was telling the truth. The plane was carrying a highly classified laser weapon. It was being transported inside a special weapons pod, a very large steel container that's airtight, watertight, bullet-proof, and so on. This key is part of the locking mechanism for the pod hatch. If there's ever an emergency, or the possibility that the pod could be lost to the enemy, the hatch can be sealed and this key then breaks away to prevent unauthorized opening of the hatch. It was somebody's idea for buying us time to recover the pod before somebody else—like this garbage collector here—can figure out how to get inside and loot the contents."

"So . . . what does that tell you?" asked Dr. Cooper.

"Oh, some good news for the U.S. government, I suppose. It means that before the plane went down, someone had time to close the hatch and seal it. That means the laser probably survived the crash and is safe and intact, even though the pod is underwater." He added in frustration, "Now if we only knew where to look."

Jay suddenly drew in a breath. Dr. Cooper looked at him, but he didn't say anything. He just looked away, troubled by his thoughts.

"What is it, son?" asked Dr. Cooper.

"I don't suppose it's worth wondering about . . ."

"What?" But then Dr. Cooper thought of it himself. "Oh . . ." He turned to Adams. "Lieutenant, just answer me a question. Would there be room for a thirteen-year-old girl in that pod, someone just a little smaller than Jay?"

Adams looked down and shook his head. "Don't even think about it, doctor. It's just too unlikely . . ."

"Is there room?"

"Doctor, you're only setting yourself up for a big disappointment—"

"Is there room?"

Adams gave up. "Yes, there's room. But it's a false hope at best. That pod's been underwater for . . . almost five days now. There just wouldn't be enough air to keep anyone alive."

"Well . . . any further discussion is pointless until we find that pod. Jerry!"

"Yes, doctor?"

"We have to ask Kolo a question."

It took some time and some persuading, but Kolo finally began to soften a little and admit that *maybe* these people weren't really pirates and spies. Adams tried to explain what the pod looked like, but Kolo didn't understand. Adams drew a picture of it in the sand, but that didn't seem to work either.

"It's big, very big," said Adams.

Jerry interpreted that to Kolo. Kolo only stared blankly and mumbled something.

"How big?" Jerry asked. "You'll have to show him."

Adams was getting impatient. He finally took a stick and began to trace out a full-size outline in the sand. "It's . . . as long as this, okay? Metal, very hard stuff, green in color, it has a big door on this end . . ." Jerry kept chattering to Kolo. "Is any of this getting through?"

Then they saw it. Suddenly Kolo understood. His eyes brightened, his mouth popped open, and he sucked in a small breath.

Jerry asked him if he'd seen the pod.

Kolo crossed his arms, set his jaw, and shook his head.

Adams threw the stick down in anger. "He's lying! He knows good and well what we're talking about!"

"Jerry," said Dr. Cooper, his voice strained, "we have to know where it is!"

Kolo only shook his head again.

Dr. Cooper went to Kolo himself and asked him, "Please tell us. We must find it."

Jerry tried to interpret Dr. Cooper's words, but Kolo just shook his head before he got the chance.

"You must understand—my daughter could be down there!"

Jerry told Kolo, but Kolo wouldn't budge.

Dr. Cooper stopped his hands only inches before they would have grabbed the little pearl diver. He was holding his breath, trying to get control of the intense feelings welling up inside him.

Jerry tried to calm him. "Dr. Cooper . . ."

"Excuse me." Dr. Cooper spun on his heels and hurried away, disappearing up the trail and into the jungle.

Adams stood close to the others and said quietly, "Don't worry. We know enough. We'll find it."

Mrs. Flaherty stole quietly up the trail, looking this way and that, floating like a bright flower among the deep green leaves. She finally came across a small clearing, and there, sitting on a log, his thoughts far away, was Jacob Cooper. She entered the clearing and approached him very gently, examining his face, reading the pain in his eyes. He had to know she was there, but he didn't look at her or acknowledge her presence at all.

She sat on the log near him, said a quick, silent prayer, then spoke very gently. "It will work out, Jacob. God is merciful."

He drew a breath, sighed it out, and tried to calm himself. "I'm sorry. I had to get away from that little man before I did something rash."

Mrs. Flaherty looked at him with wise, discerning eyes and said, "Jacob, upon my word, you're a bundle of emotion, all locked in a shell, and someday you're going to explode. I'm afraid for you."

He managed to look at her and admitted, "You are a very discerning woman, Mrs. Flaherty."

She thought for a moment, and then ventured, "It

warms me to hear you say so. But will you tell me . . . Do your heart's troubles have anything to do with Katherine?"

Dr. Cooper's face tightened immediately. "You know that's a topic I avoid, and I don't see what it has to do with our present situation."

"As you please. But it so strongly reminds me of John, my late husband. May I tell you why?"

Dr. Cooper tried to be civil. "If you wish."

"I hope you'll pardon my getting so personal, but I cared so very much for that man. There was none finer than John Flaherty. He was a godly man, full of faith and integrity, a man who loved me dearly, and I'm proud to have his name. When the Lord took him home, there was no thought I ever found harder to believe or accept."

Mrs. Flaherty paused and built up the courage to speak her next thought. "That's why I never said good-bye. I wouldn't let myself cry or feel sorrow. I wouldn't even speak his name, not ever. Perhaps I thought that if I never faced my loss, John would never really go away.

"So I guess I know how you feel and what you're going through. I know what it's like to hide yourself inside a shell and never come out. For me, the shell was my work. I traveled, I searched, I investigated, I produced for my publishers—maybe I did more in three years than in my whole life before that, and now I know why. It all kept my mind off my hurt.

"But you know, as long as you're in that shell, you can never be free. You're as much in prison . . . well, as Lila might be right now. Worst of all, if you never come out of that prison, you won't be there when those you love really need you."

Dr. Cooper relaxed. He was listening to her words. Then, in a quiet voice, he asked, "How do you know so much about me?"

"Remember our visit in Dave's boat the other night, and how you toughened up and wouldn't talk about Katherine? I knew right away you were carrying a dreadful pain deep inside. I was that way myself once." Then she cautiously added, "But you know, I could see how much Jay wanted to talk about his mother. Jacob, he wants to *feel,* he wants to love his mother's memory, he wants all of your hearts to be in touch. It hurts him to bump into that shell of yours every time he wants to reach out to you."

Dr. Cooper quietly admitted, "I've always known that to be true, even though he's never said so . . . But Lila *has* expressed herself, and quite strongly. We had a very difficult time right before she left on the plane . . ." His voice suddenly choked with emotion.

Mrs. Flaherty touched his arm. "She's in God's hands. He knows what's best. And you know what's best for you to do."

"Do I?"

She stood to leave and spoke gently to him. "A wound is never going to heal until you tend to it. Come out of that shell. Say good-bye to Katherine. *Feel.* Whether you have two children or one, they need a father whose heart they can touch. I'll be going for now."

She quietly slipped away, and Dr. Cooper remained there, pondering, praying, feeling.

A short time later, Jay was looking for his father. He thought he heard something and spotted Dr. Cooper in the clearing.

Dr. Cooper's body was turned away, and he was quietly weeping, long and steady, holding nothing back.

Jay was about to go into the clearing, but he felt a gentle hand on his shoulder.

It was Mrs. Flaherty.

"It's all right," she whispered. "He's just tending to an old wound." Then she smiled. "I'm sure he'll tell you all about it."

# ELEVEN

In the warm and comforting glow of the machine's red console lights, Lila rested, still breathing from her oxygen bottle. She had wondered from time to time how one bottle of oxygen could last so long, but finally concluded that when it ran out, it ran out. She did not want that to happen, but she was ready if it did.

She pulled her soggy little Bible from her pocket and, carefully peeling the wet, clinging pages apart, found the Book of Jonah. The sight of that tiny book in the middle of the Bible warmed her heart. For so long, it had been an interesting story, but not much more. Now Jonah, the wayward prophet, had become a close friend. Now Lila knew what he must have felt like, trapped in the belly of that great fish, and she had a far better understanding of the reason he got himself into that mess: he had tried to run from God.

"Just like me," Lila admitted to herself.

She thought back to her conversation with Lieutenant Jamison:

"Kind of like Jonah," he had said. "He tried to run from God, so God brought some trouble into his life so He and Jonah could have a talk."

"Being swallowed by the big fish, you mean," Lila replied.

"Yeah. Now *that* got Jonah's attention!"

Lila began reading Jonah's story once again. Yes, God had her attention, and as she read Jonah's prayer from inside the fish, she was touched by how much of it had become her prayer as well:

"In my distress I called to the LORD, and he answered me. From the depths of the grave I called for help, and you listened to my cry. You hurled me into the deep, into the very heart of the seas, and the currents swirled about me; all your waves and breakers swept over me. I said, 'I have been banished from your sight; yet I will look again toward your holy temple.'

"The engulfing waters threatened me, the deep surrounded me; seaweed was wrapped around my head. To the roots of the mountains I sank down; the earth beneath barred me in forever. But you brought my life up from the pit, O LORD my God.

"When my life was ebbing away, I remembered you, LORD, and my prayer rose to you, to your holy temple.

"Those who cling to worthless idols forfeit the grace that could be theirs. But I, with a song of thanksgiving, will sacrifice to you. What I have vowed I will make good. Salvation comes from the LORD."

Tears came to her eyes.

"Yes, Lord, that's me. I tried to run instead of facing my problems. I'm just sorry it took a situation like this to make me see it. Well . . . if I die, I die, but if I live . . . Lord, I'll do like Jonah said: I'll make good what I've promised. I'll do what You want me to do, and I'll get things right with Dad."

Then she felt peace in her heart, such a peace that it didn't matter that she was trapped in a sealed metal container on the bottom of the ocean. She didn't feel trapped; she didn't feel lonely. Her heart was right with God.

She laid her head down on the wooden crate and fell asleep.

The next morning, Dr. Cooper and Jay awoke with a start. The Sutolos were pounding their drums again and shouting excitedly.

"What now?" asked Jay.

Dr. Cooper was already standing at the door of their little guest hut, looking toward the beach. "Some canoes are arriving."

Jay joined his father at the door. Right across the path from them, Mrs. Flaherty had come to the door of her hut, and their neighbors, Bad Dave and Lieutenant Adams, were buffeting each other for standing room in their doorway.

As they all watched from their elevated vantage-points, a band of Sutolo warriors pulled their four big outrigger canoes onto the beach as the other Sutolos gathered around to chatter, shout, and examine whatever it was the warriors had brought.

One warrior held a metal cylinder high over his head with a shout of glee.

Lieutenant Adams recognized it immediately. "A scuba tank!"

"What do you know!" chuckled Dave.

Adams pulled on his pants and scurried down the ladder to the ground. "They've found our wrecked boat!"

Jerry Garrison was already at the beach and beckoned to them excitedly. The rest all dressed hurriedly and came on the run, working their way through the excited Sutolos to the canoes.

"Lieutenant Adams," said Jerry, "all this equipment must have come from your Navy craft!"

Adams inspected the loot in the canoes. "Yeah, you bet it did. Our diving equipment . . . tanks, masks, flippers, the works!" But he hesitated. "So now what? Do they think this is all theirs since they pulled it from the sea?"

Jerry smiled sheepishly and nodded. "But I've already talked to them about it. They say they'll be happy to loan it to you."

Adams forced a sarcastic smile. "Well, that's very nice of them." Then he spotted something else. "Oh-oh. The radio!" He pulled the small radio from the canoe and checked it. "It's ruined. Nuts! I've got to contact the *Findley*. I know they're wondering what happened to us." Adams seemed worried. "I just wish I could tell them where we are and what we know before it's too late."

"Too late?" Dr. Cooper asked with concern.

Adams seemed reluctant to say too much. "Let's just hope the rebels don't find that pod before we do."

At this moment, aboard Ivanovich's great white yacht, cruising slowly about a mile off Tukani, a watchman on the bow, thinking he spotted something in the deep blue water, shouted to the bridge. The pilot reversed the props and eased the yacht backward.

Now many of the crew—and some rebels as well—leaned over the starboard railing for a look. Some saw it and pointed, and soon all of them could make it out.

Down under the water, its outline wavy and wriggling, was a dull green section of a wing.

A whoop went up from the rebels. Ivanovich came to the railing to see it for himself. He smiled and nodded his head.

"Ah, at last!" he said in Russian. "Quickly, check the currents for the area. Lower a boat! Bridge, radio the rebels and tell them to join us here. We're getting close to the crash site!"

Three men went over the side in a small inflatable boat and motored ahead of the yacht, weaving far to one side and then the other, looking intently into the water for any other signs of the plane.

In moments they spotted another fragment and signaled the yacht. It followed them, its big engines rumbling.

Soon the rebels came speeding around the end of the island in their boat, the engine roaring at full-throttle. They were all aboard again, some of them having recovered from the Sutolo stones and sleep darts. All of them were primed and ready for the hunt.

Ivanovich returned to the bridge and clapped his hands in joy. "Too bad our American prisoners below won't be able to watch the party. To the victors go the spoils! It is only a matter of time!"

Lieutenant Adams checked out the diving equipment.

"Looks good," he said. "Tanks are still pressurized and functional. Ever done any diving, doctor?"

"Yes, quite a bit, both Jay and I."

"How about you, Dave?"

"I can outdive you any day, with or without a tank."

"So pick out a tank, all of you." Adams brought out some very large, very dangerous-looking knives. "And take one of these too, in case there's trouble. We'll get ourselves outfitted and just start looking. Jerry, we'll need your best guess where to search for Kolo's cache."

Jerry paused to think. "I know he spends a lot of time in a small atoll north of the island, but it's been a while since—"

Suddenly there was a frantic cry from up the beach. A man was running toward them, his arms waving, his face full of desperation.

It was Kolo.

"Hoo boy," said Adams, "now what?"

"I'm about to have *him* for breakfast!" said Dave.

Kolo huffed and puffed his way up to them and began to chatter excitedly. Obviously he was very upset about something.

Jerry listened and interpreted. "He says strangers have come to his secret treasure grounds. Many, many wicked men . . . a very large canoe the color of doves . . ."

"Ivanovich!" said Adams.

"They've found the crash site!" said Jay.

Jerry interpreted, "He wants us to help him, to chase the wicked men away."

Adams brightened at that. "What about the pod? Will he tell us where it is?"

Jerry babbled the question to Kolo. Kolo nodded and kept on talking.

Jerry said, "He'll show us the spot. He says it's not in the same place, that the waters have carried it further along, but the wicked men are getting very close to it."

"Can we get there before the Commies do?"

"Kolo says maybe, if we go now."

Dr. Cooper, Jay, and Dave were already loading the diving equipment into canoes. Mrs. Flaherty was rounding up oarsmen.

Adams asked Jerry, "Did Kolo see any other boats? Big gray ones? Navy ships?"

Jerry asked Kolo, then answered, "No, only the big white one, and one smaller one, probably the rebels' boat."

"I've got to contact the *Findley!*"

Just then, all of them could hear the distant rumble of an aircraft.

Jay spotted it and pointed out to sea. "There it is!"

Adams ran toward the beach for a better look. "It's one of ours, a chopper from the *Findley* on a reconnaissance run."

"All right!" said Jay. "The good guys finally got here!"

"He'll spot those rebels for sure, and maybe the pod too," said Dave.

But Adams seemed intent on only one thing. "C'mon, let's get these canoes in the water and get out there!"

Dr. Cooper asked, "Lieutenant Adams, the Navy's arriving now, and they're more than adequate to take care of the rebels. Shouldn't we wait for them to get control of the area?"

"Doctor," said Adams, "under routine circumstances that's exactly what I'd do. But this might not be routine. Now, I wouldn't bet a dime on your daughter still being alive down there, but if she is . . . We've got to get to that pod before the rebels do, and definitely before the *Findley* even gets close!"

Dr. Cooper smelled trouble. "What haven't you told us?"

"Just one more little detail, another security measure in the pod: that laser is loaded with enough explosive to vaporize the pod and everything around it. If the *Findley* even suspects that the laser might fall into enemy hands, they'll order it to self-destruct. All they have to do is make radio contact with it, and the rest is as easy as pushing a button."

"And there's no way to stop it?"

"Like I said, my radio's ruined. I can't contact them to tell them not to."

"Dad, if they see the rebels finding it . . ." Jay began.

"If they see the rebels even getting *close* to it," said Adams, "it could be all over."

Dr. Cooper had heard enough. "Let's get these canoes in the water."

With all hands pitching in, they launched out in two large canoes. Dr. Cooper, Jay, and Mrs. Flaherty rode in one, while Dave, Adams, and Kolo rode in the other. Four powerful Sutolo oarsmen in each canoe propelled their craft out through the surf, following Kolo's lead. They headed out past the shallows, then turned north, following the shoreline.

Ivanovich's yacht cruised cautiously just outside a very large atoll, the crew keeping a careful eye open for shallows and hidden reefs. Ivanovich looked across the coral island through binoculars, and suddenly his pulse quickened. He was certain he could see an oil slick, and on the far side of the shallow blue lagoon, near an almost invisible reef, a dull green surface was just poking above the water. It looked like the tail section of the plane, and there were numbers visible: MAC 502 . . . The rest was under the water.

The water here was too shallow for the big ship, so the rebels went on ahead in their boat, along with several scouts in smaller inflatables, their little engines humming like bees. As they zipped across the lagoon, they could look down into the shallow water and see the ocean floor littered with debris. Here were most of the Starlifter's remains as well as its cargo, broken and scattered everywhere in a vast, watery grave. The inflatables began to zigzag across the lagoon in search of anything that might be the laser.

Ivanovich watched their activity intently and noticed nothing else until a loud rumble from the sky drowned out the engines of the boats in the lagoon. He lowered the binoculars, looked into the sky, and then cursed loudly. A U.S. Navy helicopter! It was coming closer, and it's crew had certainly seen them!

A crewman got his attention and pointed toward the horizon. Ivanovich looked out to sea and then looked at the same scene through his binoculars.

A large Navy cruiser was heading their way.

He shouted orders to some armed guards, who

scurried below to do his bidding. In just minutes they returned, leading the captured Navy commandos at gunpoint.

"Take them forward, right out to the bow! I want them plainly visible. Let these snooping newcomers see what we have to bargain with."

The guards rudely pushed and herded the Americans forward and lined them up against the front bow railing just as the big helicopter hovered for a closer look.

Ivanovich didn't stop there. He barked some more orders to crewmen on the front deck, who uncovered a monstrous gun and swung it around, taking aim.

"Give them a warning shot!"

The gun thundered with a flash of fire and an explosion of smoke. The helicopter immediately turned and flew away.

"Ha!" laughed Ivanovich. "Take *that* message back to your ship!"

On the bridge of the *U.S.S. Findley,* the captain and his officers were watching it all while the communications officer stayed in close communication with the chopper.

"Sir," he reported to the captain, "they have Lieutenant Adams's men as hostages, with no sign of Adams. The chopper has been fired upon and is pulling back."

"Any other Americans in sight?"

"No sir—only the Soviet vessel and several small search craft belonging to the rebels."

The captain ducked into a small, dark room. Three men were inside, apparently civilians, sitting and keeping a very close eye on the complex electronic equipment that filled the room from floor to ceiling.

"Close the door, please," said one.

The captain closed the door, then spoke quietly.

"There's trouble at the crash site. The Soviets are already there in a large yacht, along with the Philippine rebels. They're scouring the area right now. They have our men and are holding them hostage."

The three men looked at each other, considering the captain's words. One asked, "Any options before we sacrifice the laser?"

"Our chopper was fired upon. We may have a real fight on our hands if we try to move in, and we can't risk the hostages," the captain answered solemnly.

"You understand our orders," said another.

"I certainly do. You may have to proceed with them."

Just then a red light came on. The three men instantly concentrated on their monitoring consoles, lights, dials, and switches.

"We have radio contact with the laser."

Beneath the deep blue waters, while boats roared to and fro far above and ships drew ever nearer, Lila lay asleep inside the pod, her head resting on the wooden crate that held the mysterious machine.

Quietly, without waking the young girl up, two amber lights on the machine's control panel suddenly turned on, adding their light to the red glow of the others.

The three men's fingers raced across rows of buttons, and their eyes scanned monitor screens as they chattered quick reports to each other.

"Positive radio response."

"Energy pack at 95 percent. That's enough power to operate."

"Armament fully functional."

One man saw something he thought a little strange. "Hmm. Someone's already switched on the circuit monitors."

"Must have been the jarring of the crash," said another.

"We're in good shape, though. All systems are functional."

"Okay," said one, throwing several switches marked with bright red warning lights. "Arming to detonate."

"Are those Soviets in for a big surprise!"

Lila awoke with a start. Her mind was fuzzy, and she wondered if she was dreaming. A whirring sound and a buzzing and a steady clicking filled the pod. Bright lights were flashing orange, red, green.

She jumped away from the crate, startled and frightened. No, she wasn't dreaming. The mysterious machine had come alive! The lights were blinking in an orderly sequence. Then, from somewhere deep inside, the machine began to hum.

# TWELVE

The Sutolo oarsmen, feeling the urgency of the situation, pulled at the oars with all their strength, and the two canoes knifed through the water with great speed, following the directions of the little pearl diver. He was pointing to a spot about a half-mile from the island. The bottom was dropping away rapidly now.

Lieutenant Adams hollered instructions to Bad Dave, Dr. Cooper, and Jay, and they all got into their diving gear, strapping on the air tanks, adjusting their diving masks, cinching up their flippers, preparing to go under. Adams had the key to the pod hatch tied to his wrist, ready for use.

Dr. Cooper checked his mask and mouthpiece, and then instructed Mrs. Flaherty, "The rebels can't be too far away. You'll have to remain above as a lookout." He handed her a spool of thin, nylon line. "I'll take one end of this line down with me. If you see trouble coming, give the line some jerks to signal me, perhaps on a scale of one to five."

"One jerk for approaching trouble, two for trouble getting closer, and five if we're really in the frying pan?"

It was a sobering thought. "Uh . . . something like that, yes. Let's just pray that things work out."

The rebels had scoured the whole lagoon and brought back to the yacht plenty of interesting canisters, crates, and bundles. But so far there was no sign of the weapons pod. Ivanovich could see the *U.S.S. Findley* in the distance, but he was not impatient—he was frantic!

"Do you see that ship?" he shouted. "Our hostages will not be effective forever. We are in a race to find that pod and escape from here before more American forces arrive. Widen the search area! Go further south, beyond the lagoon! Perhaps the current has carried more of the debris that direction."

The rebels roared away in their boat, going past the lagoon, followed by the buzzing, darting inflatables. Ivanovich shouted orders to his own crew, and the big yacht eased ahead, following at a distance.

Lila didn't know what to do, and she had no idea what the strange machine was up to. It continued to hum and blink at her, and the strange robot-head even turned this way and that a little. Could it see her? She looked the thing in the eye, but it didn't respond or follow her when she moved.

It occurred to her that someone might be controlling this thing from the outside. Sure, some kind of radio control! She took another careful look at the control panel on the side. A lot of numbers were racing over the digital displays and a lot of lights were blinking, but so far none of it made any sense. Could this thing pick up sounds?

"Hello?" she shouted. "Can you hear me?"

There was no response. The humming, clicking, and blinking just continued without skipping a beat.

Kolo was shouting and pointing downward. This was the spot. The Sutolos brought the canoes to a halt.

"Ready!" shouted Adams, and the four men put their masks and mouthpieces in place.

Adams gave his signal and fell backward into the water. Dave flopped in, then Jay.

Dr. Cooper felt a hand on his arm.

"God be with you, Jacob Cooper," said Mrs. Flaherty.

Dr. Cooper looked at her a moment, gave her a quick smile, and said, "Thank you, Meaghan Flaherty." The way he said it, he was thanking her for more than just her good wishes. He replaced his mouthpiece and went over the side.

Kolo took several deep breaths, then leaped into the water and dove into the blue depths, his legs kicking, his arms making powerful strokes.

The four divers swam down after him, moving through the warm, sky-blue water, trailing four columns of bubbles. They could see the bottom about sixty feet below them, a breathtaking landscape of brilliant coral and teeming schools of flashing fish.

Kolo reached his limit. He stopped, turned, and showed them the way, pointing beyond a coral ridge and indicating the pod was just on the other side. He gestured a farewell, and then started floating back to the surface.

The four exchanged glances through their diving masks. They were all feeling the same suspicion that Kolo might be bluffing them, but at this point there was nothing to do but continue on. They swam ahead, and Dr. Cooper kept playing out the nylon line.

Up in the canoe, Mrs. Flaherty let the spool unwind and hoped there would be enough line.

But then a Sutolo shouted and pointed.

The rebels! She could see that old familiar boat of theirs, rounding the point, swerving to and fro. They were obviously still searching for the pod. She quickly lay down in the canoe, hoping they wouldn't see her. The Sutolos were aware of the problem; they began to act like they were fishing, even though they had brought no nets.

The rebels were suspicious anyway. It didn't take them long to spot the canoes sitting there for no good reason. The rebel boat turned toward them and opened its throttle.

With danger approaching, Mrs. Flaherty gave the line one tug.

The three men aboard the *Findley* continued to communicate with the laser and passed their findings on to the captain.

"Any changes?" asked one.

"No," said the captain. "They have us in a standoff. We don't know if they've found the laser yet or not . . ."

A sudden shout came from the bridge. "Captain! They're converging on an area south of the yacht. It looks like they've found something. There are some native craft over that area right now. Looks like they're getting help from the local natives too."

The three men carefully watched their instruments.

"Keep us posted," said one. "We can blow that thing any time."

Lila was desperate. There had to be some way to send a message back to whoever was operating this machine. She studied the control panel again, trying to remember what she did last time. Oh yes! She recalled the Activate button, and then the lever that made the head move. Perhaps she could create some kind of motion the people on the outside could monitor.

She pressed the Activate button.

A deafening shriek! A brilliant shaft of red light! Lila scurried away, terrified! The robot's eye was not an eye at all, but a blinding, burning, dazzling laser! The inside of the pod was washed with red sunlight. Sparks were flying—smoke and steam were everywhere.

The divers were blinded and startled by the flashing red beam that appeared as suddenly as a lightning bolt and shone just as brilliantly, a ruby-red shaft shooting up toward the surface, cloaked in a long, foaming tube of seawater instantly turned to steam.

Water was streaming in! The laser had actually cut a hole through the pod!

Lila leaped forward and hit the Activate button again. The laser switched off.

But too late! Seawater was pouring in through a six-inch hole in the top of the pod, cascading down on Lila's head, soaking her, filling the pod.

The officers on the bridge of the *Findley* were wide-eyed. "Wow! Did you see that?"

Below, the three men were startled by their instrument readings. "The laser has fired!"

They tried to trace the cause.

"Malfunction in Laser Activation System," said one man.

"Can you correct it?" said another.

One man ran his fingers along a row of switches. "I don't see anything wrong here. It's as if the laser's getting orders from someone besides us."

"No way! Better prepare for final detonation sequence."

"Lord, deliver us!"

Mrs. Flaherty gave the nylon line three tugs. The rebels were only a short distance away now. The huge white yacht had come around the island and was closing in fast.

132

Dr. Cooper could feel the tugs and tugged in response to acknowledge them, but there was no turning back now. They had come over the coral ridge and there, lying in a hollow like a huge bottle, was the weapons pod, one end up, with a stream of bubbles escaping from a hole recently burned through it. Adams swam toward the downward end, trying to get a look at the hatch.

The boat full of rebels finally got close enough to spot Mrs. Flaherty, and at the sight of an American they roared in for the kill, yelling, hooting, and waving their rifles. The boat circled the two helpless Sutolo canoes, stirring up a huge wake that threatened to capsize them as the oarsmen struggled to keep the canoes upright. Now the inflatables were arriving, bringing still more bloodthirsty enemies. Mrs. Flaherty gave the line five desperate tugs.

Thump! Something landed in the canoe. A grenade!

Mrs. Flaherty screamed a warning to the others on her way over the side, and she and the Sutolos leaped into the water with a volley of splashes.

The grenade exploded in a plume of white water and shattered canoe fragments, the impact of the explosion knocking the Sutolos senseless.

Mrs. Flaherty felt she'd been thrown a knockout punch. She slipped in and out of consciousness, dazed, dizzy, her head spinning, her ears ringing. She tried to find the surface, but she couldn't even tell up from down.

Then her head broke the surface, and she gasped in some air. She heard shots, and bullets ripped into the water only inches from her head. She dove under the surface again. She could see the bullets zipping around her, tracing thin strings of bubbles as they cut through the water. She looked below for the divers but couldn't see them.

Ivanovich screamed orders to his crew, and the helmsman opened the throttle wide. The big yacht cut through the water, its sharp white bow aimed for the watery grave of that weapons pod.

Dr. Cooper and the others heard a splashing commotion right over their heads and looked up to see a dozen divers plunging into the water. Some were carrying metal cutting torches. Many had knives and were ready for a fight.

Strong, burly arms grabbed Mrs. Flaherty from behind! She kicked and struggled, but it was no use. The rebel diver was pulling her down, waving a knife in her face. She surrendered and even raised her hands to say so. He shoved his mouthpiece into her mouth. She took some deep breaths and gave it back. He nodded his approval of her wise behavior.

Another diver brought a spare tank and handed it to her. She began breathing from it. They held her prisoner, dragging her along, descending into the depths.

Lila was in water up to her waist, with only precious minutes left before the whole pod would be filled. With nothing to lose, she made her decision.

She grabbed her "life preserver" (the bag full of styrofoam packing) and jammed her arms through the carrying straps, securing it to her back. She clamped the oxygen mask securely to her face. Then, screaming out one last prayer, she lunged for the control panel once again, struggling and splashing her way through the rising water.

The big yacht was coming right over the pod's resting place. The helmsman eased back on the throttle as Ivanovich stepped onto the prow to watch the Sutolos fleeing in the remaining canoe, chased away by rifle fire from the rebels. Very good. Now there were only the Americans diving below, and the rebel divers would quickly take care of them.

Adams and Dave, ready for a fight, pulled their knives. But Dr. Cooper spotted the two rebels holding Mrs. Flaherty, one with a knife at her throat. Dr. Cooper and the others froze. The rebel holding the knife motioned them to swim away from the pod.

Lila had her hand on the control lever. She hit the Activate button again.

The brilliant red beam lit up the inside of the pod like crimson lightning!

All the divers were startled by the brilliant laser beam, cutting through the water like a red-hot knife, sheathed in bubbles of steam, shooting right through the walls of the pod.

With Mrs. Flaherty's captors distracted by the sight, she grabbed the opportunity—and one man's mask, tearing it from his face. He grabbed for it, which meant he had to let go of her. She unclipped his weight belt and he began to float upward, still trying to recover his mask.

The other man still held her and plunged the knife toward her. She barely managed to twist his wrist and the knife away, getting his arm into a judo hold. Now she was in a thrashing, kicking, wriggling fight for control of that blade!

Lila squinted in the brilliant light. She moved the control lever, and the robot head began to rotate. The laser beam began to sweep across the pod like a cutting torch. A sheet of water streamed in through the ever-lengthening cut.

The water quickly rose to Lila's neck.

The rebel divers backed away. Some swam for cover behind the coral and rocks. Adams and Dave swam to the ocean floor and remained there, watching that beam sweeping in a deadly arc, first pointing to one side, then rising, rising, shooting toward the surface.

Then they saw Mrs. Flaherty and her assailant, struggling, kicking, churning up the water, grappling with each other right in the path of that approaching beam!

Ivanovich heard his men screaming before he saw the laser beam himself. Suddenly, off to his left, a red thread of light as brilliant as the sun angled up out of the water, rising, rising, steeper and steeper, piercing the ocean, then the sky. High above, thin clouds dissolved as the beam burned a hole right through them.

Lila tried to hold her head above the water as she pushed the lever, forcing the laser to keep rotating. The beam continued to cut through the pod's skin, from one side, across the top, and then down the other side.

The men on the *Findley* knew what was happening.

"The laser's firing! Interrupt!"

"I can't, sir! It doesn't respond to radio commands!"

"Malfunction in the manual controls, sir."

"Detonate!"

A man hit a switch and turned a key. "Detonation sequence beginning . . . *now!* Detonation in sixty seconds."

Dr. Cooper kicked and stroked through the water and reached Mrs. Flaherty just in time, jerking both her and the rebel out of the way as the crimson beam swept right by them, heating the water enough to scald them. The rebel broke loose from Mrs. Flaherty, but now he had Dr. Cooper to contend with, and Dr. Cooper wasn't about to lose.

Ivanovich's men started screaming, and then he too realized to his horror that the laser beam was sweeping in an arc that would pass right through the yacht! He screamed to the helmsman, who put the engines in full reverse. The big yacht began to move backward.

Dr. Cooper broke the rebel's arm, and the knife tumbled to the ocean floor. The rebel backed off, holding his hand out pleadingly. He'd had enough. Dr. Cooper let him go and checked on Mrs. Flaherty. She was all right and grabbed his hand in gratitude.

The water covered Lila now, and it was rapidly heating up from the laser beam. Before too long it would cook her. The laser had almost circled the pod.

Like a razor-sharp knife, the beam came down on the yacht, slicing through the roof, the main deck, the lower deck, down to the waterline, and right through the bottom of the hull. Fires broke out. Smoke billowed from the portholes. The two halves of the yacht separated and dipped in the middle like an opened eggshell. Crewmen dove into the water in panic.

The guards holding Lieutenant Adams's men panicked and forgot their duty. The commandos were ready and quickly pounced on them, knocking them to the deck, pinning them down and taking their guns. The guards weren't interested in a fight. As soon as the commandos let go, the Russians ran for the rail and dove overboard.

Ivanovich was no better off. He clung to the rail on the bow and tried to gain some footing on the slanting deck as the yacht began to sink under him. Three Navy commandos came to his "rescue"—they took him prisoner.

Lila felt a terrific shudder and heard a metallic, grating noise. She looked up through a curtain of bubbles and debris and saw bluish light.

She gasped and pulled with her lungs, but there was nothing left! Her oxygen was gone!

"Detonation in thirty seconds."

Dave and Adams were grappling with four rebel divers. Adams disarmed one and sent him scrambling for the surface, and Bad Dave managed to use one man's skull against the other's to calm them both down.

But then every man heard a metallic sound and looked to see the upper end of the pod, cut off cleanly, drop away with a final explosion of bubbles. The laser beam disappeared, and then, to every man's shock and surprise, a small figure emerged—a struggling, kicking creature with long, blonde hair, dropping an empty oxygen bottle and swimming for the surface.

Jay's cry of joy bubbled out through his air hose as he kicked and stroked for all he was worth to reach her, with Dr. Cooper and Mrs. Flaherty not far behind.

That was all Adams needed to see. He signaled Dave to clear out, and they both swam for the surface, letting the rebels have the pod.

The rebels were satisfied with their retreat and converged on the pod like flies gathering on honey.

Lila was weakening, failing; her strokes were limp gestures. Jay got to her, grabbed her, and shoved his mouthpiece into her mouth. She began to breathe, but she was semiconscious and unaware of him.

Dr. Cooper got there and let Jay share his air as they moved quickly for the surface.

The commandos aboard the broken yacht got to a lifeboat. With great skill and speed, they lowered it and then piled in, rowing clear of the front half of the yacht as it slipped under the surface.

Dr. Cooper, Jay, and Mrs. Flaherty carefully brought Lila to the surface. Their heads no sooner broke through the water than several arms began to grab them. They began to fight—

Oh, it was Jerry Garrison!

"Come on, get in the canoe before that thing blows!"

Sutolo canoes and warriors were everywhere. Lieutenant Adams and Dave were already safe in a canoe. The Sutolos pulled Dr. Cooper into one craft and Mrs. Flaherty into another. Jay and Lila were snatched out of the water and set down gently in a third.

The ocean now became an angry hill! Suddenly, with a thunderous roar, a mountain of water rose from deep below, exploding in a vast pillar of white foam and spray. Waves washed over the canoes and soaked everyone. The Sutolos barely kept the canoes from capsizing. The ocean rolled, boiled, and foamed as rocks, coral, fish, and mud churned up from the bottom and swirled all around the canoes. On the shore, fierce waves slapped the beach again and again.

"So much for the laser-snatchers down there," said Adams.

"Captain! The chopper reports our men are safe! They've also spotted Adams, in native vessels with some American civilians!"

"All right. Let's move in and pick them up."

The ocean finally grew calm, but there was a rumbling in the sky: the helicopter from the *Findley* was returning. The broken and defeated rebels—what was left of them—fled in their motorboat, along with the men in the inflatables. The Sutolos assisted Lieutenant Adams and his men as they rounded up the floundering, struggling rebels from the sunken yacht.

Adams brought his canoe alongside to check on Lila. She was in a dazed stupor, curled up in pain. "Doctor, she has the bends, from rapid decompression. We've got to get her aboard the *Findley*."

Adams stood in the canoe and waved his arms. The helicopter lowered a sling, and they carefully put Lila in it. Dr. Cooper kissed her on the forehead before the helicopter began hoisting her skyward.

"It's a miracle we found her alive!" he said, just now beginning to believe it.

"You don't know how much of a miracle!" said Adams. "I saw that oxygen bottle she had. That bottle lasted her over five days, and those things only hold enough to last ten *minutes!*"

They watched the men on the helicopter carefully pull Lila's limp form aboard as the helicopter raced back to the *Findley*.

Adams shook his head in awe. "That's some kind of God you have there, doctor. I think your little girl's going to be all right."

# THIRTEEN

As a large jet airliner roared into the sky overhead and people, people, people rushed and bustled in all directions, an announcement came over the Tokyo International Airport's public address system:

"United Airlines, flight 203, direct to Seattle-Tacoma, is in the final boarding process. All passengers holding tickets for this flight should be aboard. This is the final call."

The announcement was repeated in Japanese, but the English was more than enough to make three people break into a run down the long concourse to the loading gate.

Dr. Cooper, a briefcase in one hand and a newspaper in the other, hurried along, with his two children on either side of him: Jay, in good shape for all the running, and Lila, completely herself again and none the worse for wear.

"What happened to our other flight?" Jay asked as they ran along.

"Canceled at the last minute," said Dr. Cooper. "I just barely got us some seats on this one, and if we don't make it, we'll have to wait until 2 in the morning."

"Let's make it, let's make it!" said Lila.

In the main lobby of the airport, an attractive and well-dressed woman looked this way and that, unable to spot a certain familiar face. She walked down the lobby to the ticketing area and checked the United Airlines flight schedule on the closed-circuit monitor.

"Oh, God help me!" she exclaimed in her Irish brogue and broke into a run, scurrying through the crowds of people, trying to get to the loading gate where a particular plane would be leaving very, very soon.

When she got there, the waiting area was empty. A lady attendant was closing the door to the loading ramp.

"Excuse me . . . this flight is all loaded?"

"Do you have a ticket, ma'am?"

"Oh, no . . . no . . ."

"How can I help you?"

"It was . . . well . . . thank you, I'll be fine." She backed away. "I just . . . I just wanted to say good-bye to someone."

"Oh, I'm sorry. I guess you're too late."

The attendant went about her business.

Mrs. Flaherty went to the big glass windows and watched as the 747 backed away from the terminal. She couldn't take her eyes off the big jet and even strained to make out a familiar face through one of the airplane's many tiny windows. But there was just no way to be sure that she was really looking at that one special man.

"Aw, Jacob, Jacob," she said quietly. "Now you're gone, and we've left so much unsaid . . ."

Aboard the taxiing 747, the Coopers watched as the flight attendant demonstrated how to fasten a seat belt, where the emergency exits were, and how to use the emergency oxygen.

Lila had said it many times since she recovered

aboard the *Findley*, but she just had to take her father's hand and say it again. "I love you, Dad."

He squeezed her hand. "I love you too. Very much."

"I'm sorry."

He chuckled. "Well, so am I. Guess we're both clear on that."

"I sure feel better now."

He smiled. Pleasant thoughts were running through his mind. "I do too. I guess you could say we've both gone through some changes."

Jay found one thought a little troubling. "Boy, it's too bad we didn't get a chance to have lunch with Mrs. Flaherty. I hope she wasn't too upset."

"Well, son, I'm hoping I was able to clear that up to her satisfaction."

Jay and Lila noticed a strange, playful smile on Dr. Cooper's face.


"Mrs. Flaherty?" came a voice behind her.

She turned. It was Colonel Griffith. "Oh, and good day to you, William."

"The orginal flight was canceled," he said with regret.

"So I found out."

"Did you get a chance to see them at all?"

She tried to smile and take it well, but the pain still showed through. "No. I was too late for that. And too late to have our lunch together too."

"I'm very sorry. I guess you all went through a lot together. It would have been nice to have a decent farewell."

"Ah . . . I guess the world's just too big, and too busy, and Jacob has places to go."

"But listen . . ." Colonel Griffith presented her with a small package. "Jake found out he wouldn't be seeing you again, so he gave this to me to give to you."

She took it and suddenly had no words.

"Go ahead. Open it."

She pulled very gingerly at the colorful wrapping that covered the little box in her hands.

Jay had never seen quite the same smile on his father's face before, and his curiosity got the best of him. "Hey, Dad, what are you thinking about?"

"Oh . . . just thinking."

Jay thought he'd explore a little. "I sure liked Mrs. Flaherty. What did you think of her?"

"Quite a woman . . . a very rare kind of woman . . . I think your mom would have liked her very much. In many ways, she's just like your mom was, a woman of deep character and strong conviction. I always admired that in Katherine."

Lila was struck by those words and had to make a mental note not to stare at her father.

Mrs. Flaherty neatly folded the wrapping and opened the lid of the little box.

Colonel Griffith saw what was inside. "What in the world . . . ?"

Mrs. Flaherty broke into a smile as she pulled a little plastic egg from the box and turned it over in her hands, just looking at it.

"A toy egg?" Griffith asked.

"Oh, you could say there's a story behind it."

She twisted the two halves of the little egg open and then began to laugh happily as she brought out what she found inside: a little paper heart.

Colonel Griffith smiled and laughed along, but then he had to admit, "I don't get it."

But Mrs. Flaherty was busy reading the note that came with the little egg:

*To Mrs. Meaghan Flaherty:*
*Unwaiting Time has forced its will upon us again.*
*Hopefully this little object lesson will say it all. Fare-*

*well for now. It is my fervent hope that somewhere in
this vast world, by God's gracious and sovereign
hand, we may soon find our paths crossing again. I
will look forward to that moment.*

*Until then, I remain sincerely yours,*
*Jacob R. Cooper, Ph.D.*

The roar of a jet shook the building with its dull
rumble, and Mrs. Flaherty looked skyward. The 747
was soaring into the air, heading for home.

She smiled and gave a little wave. "Thank you,
Jacob Cooper. Now nothing's unsaid. You've taken
good care of that."

She was ready to share an explanation with the
puzzled Colonel Griffith. "Jacob is a clever man, William. He knows how to say things so only the right
person knows what he's saying. See here? His heart
used to be in a shell. But then, I opened it. Now his
heart's free of the shell, and . . ."

Griffith smiled and ventured, "And he's given it to
*you?*"

She looked just a little shocked and unconsciously
clutched the package to her heart. "William . . . dare I
think it?"

The plane climbed to altitude and achieved level
flight. The seat belt signs turned off, and everyone
relaxed.

Lila was so quiet, Dr. Cooper had to ask, "Are you
okay?"

She looked at him and was almost afraid to say it.
"You never talked about Mom before."

He touched her cheek and looked at her a long
moment. Then, with a new light in his eyes, he said,
"Then let's talk."

And they did, all three of them, for hours on end,
high over the Pacific, bound for home.